"It's obvious someb___
want us to be toget___
they're playing dirty. What we need to do
is stand united. I want you to come to me
if anything like this happens again. Deal?"

"Deal," she replied.

"Do you want me to call Dillon?"

"No." The idea of anyone else knowing about this totally appalled her. "I'm sure the person who put that in the mailbox didn't leave any fingerprints or anything else that might help identify them. There's really nothing Dillon can do, and I would prefer that nobody know about this."

"Lily, I will never, ever cheat on you or do anything to dishonor you. I swear to you I'm just not that kind of man."

In the very depths of her heart she believed him. But trust had only just begun to build with her, and it had been far easier to doubt him.

"I'm sorry, Jerod. I'm sorry I doubted you," she said. "I just saw what was in the package and I felt so betrayed...so angry that I couldn't even think straight."

* * *

Don't miss the other exciting romances in the Cowboys of Holiday Ranch miniseries!

* * *

If you're on Twitter, tell us what you think of Harlequin Romantic Suspense! #harlequinromsuspense

Dear Reader,

What would you do to gain your heart's desire? If what you really wanted in life was a partner and a child, to what lengths would you go? Like the television shows now popular, would you marry a stranger? Meet a person who lived overseas and become a ninety-day fiancée? Or maybe you'd marry your best friend and hope that romance might grow.

Jerod Steen is one of the last two original cowboys at the Holiday Ranch who hasn't found love and marriage. More than anything Jerod wants a child of his own, and he comes up with a plan to get what he wants...with unexpected consequences!

I hope you all enjoy reading Jerod's journey as much as I loved writing it.

Thanks for reading!

Carla Cassidy

THE COWBOY'S TARGETED BRIDE

Carla Cassidy

HARLEQUIN®
ROMANTIC SUSPENSE™

Recycling programs
for this product may
not exist in your area.

ISBN-13: 978-1-335-62678-3

The Cowboy's Targeted Bride

Copyright © 2020 by Carla Bracale

This edition published by arrangement with Harlequin Books S.A.

For questions and comments about the quality of this book, please contact us at CustomerService@Harlequin.com.

Harlequin Enterprises ULC
22 Adelaide St. West, 40th Floor
Toronto, Ontario M5H 4E3, Canada
www.Harlequin.com

Printed in U.S.A.

Carla Cassidy is an award-winning, *New York Times* bestselling author who has written over 170 books, including 150 for Harlequin. She has won the Centennial Award from Romance Writers of America. Most recently she won the 2019 Write Touch Readers Award for her Harlequin Intrigue title *Desperate Strangers*. Carla believes the only thing better than curling up with a good book is sitting down at the computer with a good story to write.

Books by Carla Cassidy

Harlequin Romantic Suspense

Cowboys of Holiday Ranch

A Real Cowboy
Cowboy of Interest
Cowboy Under Fire
Cowboy at Arms
Operation Cowboy Daddy
Killer Cowboy
Sheltered by the Cowboy
Guardian Cowboy
Cowboy Defender
Cowboy's Vow to Protect
The Cowboy's Targeted Bride

Colton 911

Colton 911: Target in Jeopardy

The Coltons of Red Ridge

The Colton Cowboy

The Coltons of Shadow Creek

Colton's Secret Son

Visit the Author Profile page at Harlequin.com for more titles.

Chapter 1

"Tricia is pregnant again." Dusty Crawford's face beamed with happiness.

"Congratulations, you lucky devil." A punch of yearning hit Jerod Steen right in the pit of his belly.

The two cowboys sat in the Bitterroot café enjoying a rare lunch together. They had been sent into town on separate errands and had decided to grab a quick lunch together while they were out.

"We're hoping for a girl this time," Dusty said.

"That would be nice. I would love to have a kid," Jerod replied. "Lately I've been thinking about it all the time. I'm more than ready to be a father."

"Aren't you missing an important ingredient?" Dusty raised a blond eyebrow with amusement.

Jerod laughed drily. "Yeah, and that is a problem."

Dusty took a bite of his burger and eyed his friend as he chewed. "You seem to date off and on. None of those women have caught your fancy?"

Jerod shook his head. "I really don't date that much, and nobody I've seen or spent any time with has made me want to jump into marriage with them. I know the kind of woman I want to spend my life with and to have a family with, and none of those women has been right."

Dusty chewed some more and then took a drink of his soda. "Maybe you could pay some woman to be one of those surrogates. You know, you pay their expenses and then some and they would carry your baby and then give it to you."

Once again Jerod shook his head. "That's not what I want. I want my child to have both a mother and a father. I want a marriage so my kid will know the security of having two loving parents in a home."

He reached up and touched the scar that raced down the side of his face, a permanent reminder of the last time he'd seen his mother. He'd been fifteen years old, and he'd never seen her again. There had never been a place in her life for him, and he'd never known his father. He wanted better for himself and any children he'd have.

He grabbed a French fry from his plate and popped it into his mouth, dismissing thoughts of his mother. When it came time for him to have a child, he'd make sure to pick a very different kind of woman than the one who had given birth to him.

"I don't know what to tell you, buddy," Dusty said. "Maybe you need to sign on to one of those internet dating sites. Who knows, maybe you'll find a perfect match there."

"No way," Jerod replied firmly. "On most days I don't even like to answer my cell phone. There's no way I want to date through it."

Dusty laughed. "I hear you on that."

"I just feel like time is passing me by, and I don't want to be an old-man father," Jerod said.

Dusty laughed once again. "Jerod, you're not exactly ready for the grave yet."

"I'm thirty-five. That's ancient in father years."

"I'd think you get your kid fix working at the community center."

"I love my work there, but those aren't my kids, and it's not the same. I want a baby to raise from birth." For the past three years, Jerod had worked with some of the youth in town a couple of evenings a week. Most of the kids only had one parent in the home, or their parents worked in the evenings and the time at the community center for the kids helped take up some of the slack for the parents.

A lot of his time there was spent with several fatherless boys who needed a male mentor in their lives. And while Jerod found it very rewarding, it didn't take the place of his desire to start his own family.

"Maybe you need to start spending your time off in Oklahoma City. The dating pool there has to be bigger than it is here in Bitterroot," Dusty said.

"Maybe," Jerod replied without conviction. Dating in a city a couple hours away definitely wasn't an ideal situation. Bitterroot, Oklahoma, was a small town, but Jerod wished he could find his perfect woman here, where he lived and worked.

Thankfully, the topic of conversation changed to things that needed to be done at the ranch, and by that time they'd finished eating. The two of them left the café and walked outside and into the brisk, cool October air.

"Won't be long before winter will be here," Dusty said.

"Yeah, I know." It would be another long, lonely winter, Jerod thought.

"I'm heading to the grocery store to pick up supplies for Cookie," Dusty said. Cord Cully, aka Cookie, was the cook at the ranch.

"You'd better hurry—you know how Cookie gets if he thinks you dawdled in town."

Dusty laughed. "He can be a cantankerous old coot."

"Yeah, but the man definitely knows how to cook. I'm going to the feed store, but first I need to head to the bank and get some cash out," Jerod said. "I just spent the last of my pocket money on lunch."

"Then I'll see you back at the ranch." As Dusty turned to head to the grocery store, Jerod went the opposite direction toward the bank. While he walked, he tried to dismiss the depression that had fallen over him.

For the past couple of years, he'd watched his fellow cowboys at the Holiday Ranch fall in love, get married and start families of their own, and while Jerod was happy for all of them, he yearned for the same thing for himself.

He pushed these thoughts aside as he entered the bank lobby. There was only one teller working, and he was currently occupied talking to Lily Kidwell.

Jerod knew Lily because her nine-year-old son, Caleb, came to the community center a couple evenings a week. Caleb was a good kid but had some anger issues, and there had been times Jerod had driven out to the Kidwell ranch to discuss Caleb's behavior with Lily. Standing behind her in line, he couldn't help but hear her conversation with Larry Graham, the teller.

"Please, Larry, go back again and tell her I really need to speak with her," she said. Jerod assumed Lily was talking about Margery Martin, the bank president.

Margery was a snooty old maid who enjoyed wielding financial power over people and was known as one of the town's biggest gossips. Jerod had little respect for the older woman.

"I can't go back and ask her again," Larry said to Lily. "I've already asked her twice, and she's adamant she doesn't want to speak with you. I'm sorry, Ms. Kidwell."

"Then please just give her a message that I need another month...just one more month. I swear I should be able to pay the mortgage up in the next month, but tell her please not to foreclose on me." Lily's voice was filled with a desperate appeal. She reached up and tugged on the ends of her thick brown hair, a nervous gesture Jerod recognized from the few occasions when he'd talked to her about her son.

"I'll give her the message, but that's really all I can do for you," Larry replied in obvious sympathy.

"Thanks, Larry. I appreciate it." Lily turned and saw Jerod. Her cheeks instantly turned pink. "Oh hi, Jerod," she said.

"Hey, Lily. How are you doing?" He smiled, hoping she didn't realize he'd overheard her conversation with Larry. He knew it would greatly embarrass her for him to know her personal business. She'd always seemed like a private person.

"I'm doing just fine," she replied and flashed him a quick smile that didn't quite reach the blue of her eyes. "I've got errands to run and I'm on my lunch hour from school, so I'll see you around later."

She scooted out of the bank as if her black slacks were on fire. Despite speaking to Lily about her son, Jerod didn't know much about her. She was a respected teacher at the elementary school, and he knew she had a spread south of town, where she lived alone with Caleb. And now he knew she was apparently having some very serious financial troubles.

Not his problem, he told himself as he conducted his bank business and then headed for the feed store. He dismissed all thoughts of Lily Kidwell as he finished his errands in town and then drove back to the Holiday Ranch.

When he turned in to the ranch entrance, he felt the usual sense of homecoming. This had been his home since he was fifteen. At that time the place had been owned by Cass Holiday, otherwise known as Big Cass.

When Cass's husband had died, most of her

ranch hands had left, not believing that she was strong enough or smart enough to run the big spread. With the help of a social worker, Cass had wound up staffing her ranch with a dozen runaway boys who were living on the streets and looking for a better life.

They had all come from abusive backgrounds, and initially they had been mistrustful of the tough-talking woman and most of them had no self-worth at all. But it had been a match made in heaven. The boys had developed a brotherly bond with each other and had become fiercely loyal to Big Cass. Unfortunately she'd been killed in a tornado that had swept the area several years ago, but she'd left the ranch to her niece, Cassie, and the cowboys had all bonded to her, as well.

He parked his truck in the big shed and then walked the short distance to what they all referred to as the cowboy motel. Each of the dozen men had his own small room in the building, and in the back was the dining/rec room.

He headed to the dining room now. The men should all be finishing up with their lunches now. Most of them were still there. They all greeted him as he walked in, and he slid into a seat at the table next to his closest friend, Mac McBride.

Of the original twelve boys who had come here from the streets, one was dead, and the others had all married. Mac and Jerod were the only bachelors left.

"Hey, man, what's up?" Mac greeted him.

"Not much."

"You going to fill a plate before Cookie starts putting things away?"

"Nah, Dusty and I grabbed lunch at the café," Jerod replied. "Anything new here?"

"Yeah, you were voted to muck out the horse stalls this afternoon," Mac said with a grin. "You know when you're gone for a while, that's what happens."

Jerod laughed. "I read the work schedule this morning, and I know that particular job was assigned to you. I'm on horseback this afternoon checking out the herd."

Mac grinned. "Well, it was worth a try."

Jerod waited until Mac had finished eating, and then the two of them left the dining room and went their separate ways for their chores. Minutes later Jerod was saddled up on his horse and headed out to the pasture.

Autumn was his favorite time of year. He'd arrived here in the fall, when the leaves were beautiful oranges and reds. Even though he'd been scared to death, he'd harbored the hope that Big Cass and this ranch could offer him a better life than living on the streets.

Although the social worker, Francine Rogers,

had tried to talk all of the runaways into returning to their homes and reuniting with their parents, none of the young boys had seen that as an option. So she'd brought each of them here to Big Cass.

He'd known nothing about being a working cowboy, but Cass had been a patient and sometimes tough teacher, and now Jerod couldn't imagine doing anything else. He loved the smell of the pastures and working with the livestock. As much as he enjoyed living and working here, his real dream was to have his own place.

A vision of Lily Kidwell suddenly filled his mind. She wasn't a beautiful woman, although he found her pleasant enough to look at. She had kind blue eyes and ordinary shoulder-length brown hair. She was slender, but he'd never seen her without a worried frown creasing her forehead. He also knew she was involved in charity work.

He'd never considered her as a romantic partner. As far as he knew, she didn't date at all. He had no idea who her son's father was, but it was apparent the man hadn't been in the picture for years.

And she might be losing her ranch.

Maybe he could… No, it was way too crazy to even consider. He tried to dismiss the wild idea out of his head, but surprisingly, it lingered. Jerod had never been much of a risk taker in his life. He was a hard worker, a steady and reliable man.

He didn't do wild and crazy things, so why was he even entertaining a wild and crazy idea now? Apparently his conversation with Dusty at lunchtime had completely addled his brain.

A gust of wind caught the underside of his black cowboy hat. Before it blew from his head, he slammed his hand on top to set it down more firmly. Now it was time to put silly ideas away and focus on his job.

Lily Kidwell walked out of the Bitterroot Elementary School and into the brisk October air. After the debacle at the bank that had occurred during her lunch hour, she was just eager to get home. Normally she'd be walking out with her nine-year-old son, Caleb. However, today Caleb was being picked up by a friend's father so the two boys could work on a science project together.

"Hey, Lily...wait up."

She turned to see her best friend and fellow teacher, Krista McNight, hurrying toward her. "You sure are in a hurry," she said as she caught up with Lily. The two had been best friends since Lily had moved to Bitterroot and started teaching at the school.

In the past ten years, they had been there for each other during a lot of good and bad things. Krista had been there for her when Cody had walked out on her, and Lily had been there for her friend when her husband had divorced her and they'd begun a coparenting arrangement that left Krista frustrated most of the time. The one thing Lily hadn't shared with her friend was the ugly state of her finances.

"I'm just tired and ready to get home and relax," Lily replied.

"Where's Caleb?" Krista asked.

"He went home with Benny Granger's father to work on the boys' science fair project. I'm supposed to pick him up there at six thirty. What about you? Where is Henry?" she asked, referring to Krista's nine-year-old son.

"At Jimmy Richland's place, working on their science fair project." Krista laughed, and her bright blue eyes sparkled with humor. "The science fair has taken on a life of its own."

"A little over three weeks and it will all be over," Lily replied. "Did you volunteer to work that night?"

"Not me. I get enough of the kids during regular school hours. What about you?"

"I'm working the fair," Lily replied. "I figured Caleb was going to be there anyway, so I might as well help out."

"With both of our boys occupied for a little while, do you want to stop by the Watering Hole on the way home and grab a drink?" Krista asked. She flipped her bleached-blond hair over her shoulder. "Maybe we can find a couple of good-looking cowboys to buy us a drink."

Lily laughed. "You know I don't roll that way." She knew Krista spent quite a bit of time at the popular bar with some of the other teachers both after school and on the weekends, but Lily had only gone with them a couple of times.

"You're never any fun, Lil," Krista said with a pout.

Lily laughed again. "That's me, just plain old boring Lily."

"Oh, you know I didn't mean it that way," Krista hurriedly replied.

"I'm still taking my boring butt home now so I can relax awhile before I need to pick up Caleb."

"Then I'll just see you tomorrow morning."

The two women said their goodbyes and then parted to go to their cars. As Lily drove toward home, she tried to empty her mind and just enjoy the drive, but it was impossible not to think about her dire financial situation.

A heavy wave of hopelessness descended on her shoulders. It was looking like it was going to be impossible for her to hang on to the land, on to the house she had bought a little over ten years ago.

She couldn't believe it was coming down to this. All her hard work, all her hopes and dreams of having this ranch to eventually hand over to her son when he was old enough, were crashing down around her.

An old resentment threatened to surge up inside her. Damn Cody Lee, wherever he was. When she'd bought her place, he'd promised to work it with her. He'd also promised to love her and to be by her side forever. All lies.

She shut down any further thoughts of Cody. They only reminded her that she would never, ever trust a man or love again. Her finances weren't going to change, and she definitely couldn't change the past. The only thing she was grateful for was that Cody had given her Caleb.

Still, as she pulled down the long driveway to her house, her love for her home buoyed up inside her. The three-bedroom ranch house was painted white with forest-green shutters and trim, and it was flanked by large trees on either side that now sported beautiful orange, gold and red leaves.

Some distance away from the house were the barn and several outbuildings. This had been her home for ten years and she loved it here. But now she was terrified that she would lose it all.

She parked and went into the house and carried the papers she'd brought home to grade to the kitchen table. She then made herself a cup of hot tea and sank down to work on her third graders' papers. She loved teaching, but it had never been her first choice for what she wanted to do with her life. She'd only gotten her teaching degree as a backup plan.

She'd wanted to be a rancher, and when she'd bought this place, she'd believed she and Cody would work this ranch together. They'd raise cattle and kids. But that dream had died when she'd gotten pregnant and Cody had immediately disappeared from her life, along with most of the money she'd saved up and had in her bank account.

By the time she'd graded all the papers, it was time for her to head back into town to pick up Caleb from his friend's house. Minutes later Caleb was in the truck and they were heading back home.

The conversation revolved around the project the two boys were working on, and once they got home, he sat at the kitchen table and did his homework while she cooked, and then they ate dinner.

After that, they cleared the dishes together, and then Caleb went back to his bedroom to play video games before bedtime. Lily sank down on the sofa. It wasn't long before she headed down the hallway to Caleb's bedroom. She knocked and then opened his door. He was on the bed playing a car-racing game.

"Hey, buddy. Are you winning?"

Caleb paused the game. "I keep getting almost to the end, but before I get there I crash and burn."

"So, you need to practice more on your driving skills before I let you drive my car," she replied teasingly. Caleb's brown hair shone with gold highlights. He had beautiful blue eyes and she thought he was a good-looking boy. She knew she might be biased, but she'd had others comment on his handsomeness.

Caleb now flashed her his beautiful smile. "I can't wait until I'm old enough to drive your car."

Lily laughed. "You've got a way to go. And now you have fifteen minutes and then it's time for lights out."

"You make me go to bed so early," he grumbled.

"Boys need plenty of sleep to grow big and strong and do well in school." She walked over to him, swiped his unruly brown hair off his forehead and kissed him. "I'll be back in fifteen minutes."

She left his room and went into the living room and sank down on the sofa. Caleb was her very heart and soul, but lately she'd been worried about him. He had started displaying some anger issues, and she didn't know where they came from. He'd been in trouble both in school and at the community center a couple of times for fighting or disorderly conduct, and she had no idea what he was so angry about.

She had tried to get him to talk to her about

anything that might be troubling him, but he absolutely refused. She had also hoped that he might confide in Jerod Steen, who was a strong male role model at the community center where Caleb went a couple of evenings a week, but that hadn't happened, either.

Her cheeks now burned with remembered embarrassment as she thought of Jerod. She was relatively sure he had overheard her conversation with Larry at the bank earlier that day. It was embarrassing enough to find herself in such financial straits, but it was even worse that somebody else now knew about it.

She'd already arranged to sell a lot of her Hereford steers to the stockyard in Oklahoma City in two weeks, which would give her the money to at least catch up on the mortgage. But Margery Martin, the president of the bank, could be a real witch, and she'd already warned Lily of impending foreclosure proceedings.

Lily worried that she didn't have two weeks left before Margery lowered the boom. Even if Lily was able to catch up on the payments, there was always going to be another payment…and another…and another. Her teaching pay wasn't enough to do everything.

With a deep sigh, she returned to Caleb's bedroom. "Time for lights-out, Caleb."

"I know." He turned off his game and then

snuggled down beneath his sheets. She sank down on the edge of the twin bed with him, grateful that he really rarely fought her about bedtime. He could be such a good boy, and she wished she could help him with his anger issues.

"Good night, my sweet boy," she said and pulled the sheets up closer around his neck.

"Good night, my sweet mother," he replied with a giggle and wrapped his arms around her neck and gave her a big hug.

She cherished these moments of closeness with him, which were becoming rarer as Caleb got older. He held her for just a few seconds and then released her. She deposited another kiss on his forehead and then got up. "Sweet dreams," she said and then left his room.

She went into the kitchen and made herself a cup of hot tea, then carried it into the living room and sank down on the sofa. She was exhausted but too stressed out to go to bed so early.

A weary sigh escaped her. She only had one ranch hand, because there wasn't enough money to hire more. She knew in order for the place to be really successful she needed to throw more money at it, but at the moment she was living hand to mouth.

She'd only taken a couple of sips of her tea when she heard the crunch of gravel outside, indicating somebody had just pulled up.

She got up and moved to the window. She pulled the curtain aside and mentally groaned as she saw Jerod's familiar truck parked outside. What now? Caleb had been at the community center the evening before. Had he caused trouble? Gotten into another fight?

She moved to the front door and opened it just as Jerod stepped up on her front porch. "Jerod," she greeted him.

"Hi, Lily. I know it's rather late, but could I come in and speak with you for a few minutes?"

"Of course." She opened the door wider so he could enter. He brought with him the scents of fresh air and a faint fragrance of a pleasant cologne. She closed the door behind him and then gestured him to the sofa.

She sat next to him and turned to face him. "What has he done now?" she asked with a sense of dread.

"Actually, I'm not here about Caleb," he replied.

She looked at him in surprise. The only time she'd ever had any interaction with Jerod had been when he'd spoken to her about Caleb losing his temper at the community center.

She certainly wasn't immune to the fact that Jerod was a very good-looking man. His thick dark brown hair was slightly shaggy and his eyes were the color of rich chocolate. Still, the scar that ran down the side of his face and the fact that he seemed stingy with his smiles made him look hard and unapproachable, although she knew the boys he worked with adored him.

He was a tall and slim man, but with broad shoulders and big biceps that spoke of strength. There was an air of confidence to him that added to his attractiveness.

"Then why are you here?" she asked.

"I couldn't help but overhear your conversation this morning at the bank."

Her cheeks flamed hot. "I'm so embarrassed that you heard that."

"There's nothing to be embarrassed about. We all go through hard times," he replied.

"Yes, but unfortunately I don't see a real end to my hard times," she confessed.

"I know you work as a teacher. I also know you have some good pasture here. Who is working your ranch for you?" he asked.

"Right now I only have one ranch hand, Rod Landers."

Jerod frowned. "How is he working out for you?"

She shrugged. "Better than nobody. He's a nice guy and seems very loyal to me." She looked at him curiously. "Why are you asking me all this? If you want a job here, I'm certain I can't afford you."

He shifted positions and gazed at a point just over her head. Was he nervous about something?

Why was he really here? What did he want? She waited for him to tell her.

"I'm looking for something a little more permanent than to be a ranch hand for you," he finally said.

She frowned in confusion. "More permanent? I don't understand. What do you mean?"

His gaze met hers again. "There's something I want that I think you can give me, and in return I can save your ranch."

She was even more confused now than she had been. "Jerod, what are you talking about?"

"I want a family, and I want a child of my own. What I'm proposing to you is a marriage of convenience. We get married, you give me a child and I'll work hard to turn your ranch around, but I'd want us to stay married so my child would be born and raised in a real family, and I would accept Caleb as my own son."

Lily stared at him in stunned surprise. Was he really serious? Or was he completely insane?

Chapter 2

"Jerod… I… I don't even know what to say. Are you being serious, or is this some kind of a joke?"

A deep embarrassment swept through Jerod. What on earth had he been thinking to come here and actually voice his crazy idea out loud to Lily? He immediately got to his feet.

"Never mind, Lily. It…it was just a stupid idea. I just assumed you had nobody in your life and I don't have anyone in mine and maybe we could help each other out. Just forget it. Forget I was even here."

Before she could say another word to him, Jerod practically ran out of the house. Once he was in his truck and heading back to the ranch, he cursed himself for acting on his insane idea.

He'd stewed on his plan all afternoon and into the early evening and had somehow convinced himself it wasn't such a crazy idea after all. Thankfully he hadn't told anyone back at the ranch what he was going to do. If the other cowboys got wind of what he'd just done, they'd laugh him clear out of town.

Lily probably thought he had a screw loose to even broach this with her. God, he wished he could take back what he'd just done. Now it was really going to be awkward whenever he ran into her or had to speak to her about her son.

When he returned to the ranch, he went straight to his room rather than going to the rec room to socialize. He really didn't feel like talking to anyone. He just wanted to mentally kick his own butt for being so damned stupid.

Over the next two days, he worked hard on the ranch and tried to forget he'd ever made the stupid proposition to Lily. Thankfully, he hadn't seen her since he'd embarrassed himself in front of her.

He was now seated at the dinner table with Mac on one side and Donnie Brighton on the other. Donnie had been hired about six months ago. He was good-natured and got along with everyone. He was also a hard worker who took pride in doing a good job. He'd immediately been a good fit with the other cowboys.

"Thankfully, we've managed to have a stretch of peace when it comes to the Humeses' men," Mac said.

"Let's don't tempt fate by even talking about them," Jerod replied.

The ranch next to the Holiday spread was owned by a man named Raymond Humes. Raymond was a vindictive old man who had hated Big Cass, and his ranch hands continued to stir up trouble for the Holiday Ranch. There had been intentionally set fires and downed fencing and cattle stealing. The Humeses' men were responsible, but they were rarely arrested because of a lack of hard evidence.

"Whenever I get my own place, I'll make sure the neighbors are friendly and there's no mean-hearted people like Humes's men living next to me," Jerod added.

Donnie raised an eyebrow. "Are you thinking of moving on from here?"

"Eventually I'd like to have my own spread," Jerod replied. "But I'm not leaving anytime today or tomorrow."

"Well, that's good," Donnie replied and then turned his attention to Mac. "Hey, I saw a flyer announcing that the Croakin' Frog band is playing at the Watering Hole this Saturday night. Are you playing with them?"

"Yeah, they asked me to join them for the night," Mac replied.

Mac had an amazing singing voice, and many evenings when the cowboys gathered in the rec room he entertained them by singing and strumming his guitar. Mac was also the resident horse whisperer. He was in charge of breaking and training horses that Cassie bought, and he often worked with other horses that ranchers around the area brought to him.

"Do you ever think of joining the Croakin' Frog band permanently?" Donnie asked Mac.

"Nah. They travel a bit, and I haven't wanted to do that. Besides, playing my music and singing for you guys is enough for me," Mac replied.

Maybe this was what the rest of his life would look like, Jerod thought as he listened to Mac and Donnie talk. Good friends and good food, evenings spent listening to Mac's music…maybe this was all Jerod could expect for the rest of his life.

It would be a pleasant life, much better than he'd ever dreamed of when he'd been fifteen and had run out of a seedy motel room, bloodied by his mother. Yes, it was a good life here on the Holiday Ranch. He just wanted more.

After dinner and cleanup, they moved from the eating area to the sofas and chairs in another part of the same room. This space also had bookshelves filled with books and a television that was rarely turned on.

Seven of them settled in as Mac picked up his guitar and began to strum a tune. Jerod relaxed back into the sofa, enjoying the sense of brotherhood that always accompanied these evenings.

Mac had only been playing for a few minutes when another one of the new cowboys, Jeff Haggarty, walked into the room. They all greeted him, and then he directed his attention to Jerod. "When I was headed here from my room, there was a lady knocking on your door. I told her you were probably back here and I'd get you for her."

"Oh, okay." Jerod got to his feet amid hoots and teasing from the other men. It could only be one woman knocking at his door, and he could only imagine why she was here. He could guess that Lily had stewed on his proposition for a while and was probably here to twist his hat into a million knots for even thinking she was the kind of woman who would be interested in his crazy idea.

And he wouldn't blame her. It had been completely inappropriate for him to voice such a harebrained idea to her. He left the building to walk around to the cowboy rooms on legs that moved in dread. He definitely wasn't looking forward to facing her once again.

He turned the corner, and there she was, standing in front of his door. She was clad in a pair of jeans that hugged her slender legs and a bulky black sweater. Her features were completely unreadable as she watched his approach.

"Lily," he greeted her.

Immediately one of her hands reached up and twirled a strand of her hair, letting him know that she was nervous. "Hi, Jerod." Her gaze darted around the area. "Uh…is it possible we could go someplace private and talk? Maybe we could go into your room and have a private conversation?"

"Okay," he replied with surprise. This was the very last thing he'd expected from her. Maybe she just wanted to berate him in the privacy of his own home.

He opened his room door, grateful that he was a neat man. His twin bed was made up with the navy spread, and the top of his chest of drawers and nightstand were dust-free. He pulled a folding chair out of his small closet and opened it, assuming she might not feel comfortable with both of them sitting on the narrow bed.

"Thank you," she said and sat in the chair. He sat across from her on the edge of the bed and looked at her expectantly, unsure what might happen next.

"Jerod, I've been thinking about what you said to me the other night," she began.

"I'm sorry, Lily. I was way out of line," he replied. "I should have never come to you like I did."

"So, you didn't mean it?"

It was impossible for him to know what she was thinking. He didn't really know her, and right now her features gave nothing away. "Oh, I did mean it." Why was she here?

"Then I'd like to talk to you about it. Uh…if I would agree to it, I wouldn't want anyone else to know about the arrangement," she said.

Jerod's heart quickened. Was she actually considering accepting his proposition?

"I would want everyone to believe that we've been secretly dating for months and that we're marrying because we're in love with each other." Her cheeks grew pink and she cast her gaze to the nearby wall. "That's the only way I would even consider doing this."

"I don't have a problem with that," he replied, and his heartbeat accelerated even more. He felt as if he was in an alternate universe and suddenly anything was possible.

She looked down at her hands, which were twisted together in her lap. "I feel like if we do this, then I'm somehow prostituting myself to save my ranch."

"Oh God, Lily, I never meant for you to feel that way," he replied, appalled by what she'd just voiced.

"I know you didn't, and the only reason I might consider this is, aside from you saving the ranch, I've always wanted another baby." Once again color leaped into her cheeks. "And if we did this and I had a baby, then I would want your promise that you would never, ever take that baby away from me."

"I would never do that to you, and more importantly, I wouldn't do that to the child. But I'm not going into this with a divorce as an option."

She released a small, nervous laugh. "I can't believe I'm considering this. But the truth is I'm in trouble with the ranch and I would do anything to save it for my son."

"I don't want to pressure you in any way, Lily. I do want you to understand that what I'm offering is a marriage that will last through time. We're both two mature adults who should be able to form a working partnership for the sake of Caleb and any other children we might have."

"I'm certainly not interested in getting married and then divorcing," she replied. "I came from a broken marriage, and I wouldn't wish that on any child. If we have issues, I would expect us to do whatever possible to get through them together."

"I'm in complete agreement," he replied.

"I assume it would be just a small ceremony at the justice of the peace's office."

Jerod thought he heard a touch of regret in her voice. "Will this be your first marriage?"

She nodded. "Caleb's father and I never married."

He'd talked enough to his fellow cowboys to know that most women wanted some sort of a ceremony for their wedding that included a white dress and beautiful flowers and a reception for friends and family.

"You know, we could probably pull together a fine wedding in a week or two in Cassie's barn."

Her blue eyes lit up a bit. "Really?"

"You just get your dress and give me the time and date and I'll take care of the rest," he said with more confidence than he felt.

"Shall we say a week from this Saturday?" Her hands immediately began to twist together again.

"And the following Monday, we'll go in to the bank together, and I'll make things right on your mortgage."

She immediately popped up out of the chair. "You should have my phone number since you've called me about Caleb before. Would you mind giving me yours?" She dug into her purse, grabbed her phone and held it out to him.

He stood from the bed, and as he took the phone from her he couldn't help but notice that her fingers trembled. "Lily, don't do this if you have any doubts at all."

She laughed wryly, her laughter surprisingly pleasant to hear. "Jerod, I wouldn't be human if I didn't have any doubts about this. But I'm throwing caution to the wind. I loved Caleb's father and that didn't work out so well. Perhaps a partnership without love is exactly what I need for the rest of my life."

She held Jerod's gaze for a long moment and then looked away. He programed his number into her contacts and then handed her phone back to her. "How much of this are you going to tell Caleb?" he asked.

"None of it. I want him to believe we fell in love and are getting married. Just because I don't believe in love anymore doesn't mean I want him not to believe in it." She walked over to the door.

"Then how about I give you a call tomorrow and we can talk more about specifics?"

"I'm usually home from work by four, so any time after that would be fine."

Minutes later Jerod stood in the middle of his room, his heart still beating an unsteady rhythm. He couldn't believe Lily had just agreed to his plan. Apparently his insanity was contagious.

There was no question that excited adrenaline flowed through his veins. Was he finally going to get what he wanted? A family of his own? It would have been nice if there had been true, undying love involved, but he wasn't upset that there wasn't.

He could respect and care about Lily. He could be her very best friend, the person she leaned on, and he would work to gain Caleb's trust and respect in his role as stepfather.

He definitely needed to have a heart-to-heart with Dusty and Mac. They were the only people who could blow up the whole thing by telling even a single person that Jerod and Lily hadn't been dating. He trusted his friends to keep the secret, but Jerod definitely needed to talk to them both so they were all on the same page.

What he needed to do right now was calm down enough to get a good night's sleep. He only hoped Cassie would not only lend him her barn, but also help him pull together a wedding in record time.

Was this really going to happen, or would Lily realize just how crazy this scheme was and change her mind before sunrise tomorrow?

Lily drove away from the Holiday Ranch with her stomach muscles jumping all around in nervous spasms. What had she just done? Had she lost her mind? Had the stress in her life finally sent her into complete insanity?

Initially she'd rejected Jerod's proposal outright as the most outlandish thing she'd ever heard. But the more she thought about it, the less crazy it had sounded. She'd finally convinced herself that maybe it was the best thing that would ever happen to her.

Her ranch would be saved, she and Jerod could build a future and a new family together, and Caleb would have a strong male figure in his life full-time. It sounded like a win-win for everyone.

But it was insane. It felt something like an arranged marriage from bygone days. Only in this case it wasn't parents making their daughter marry a man she didn't know to solidify their family fortune, it was her doing it to herself.

She'd never heard anything bad about Jerod Steen, and in a town where gossip was as common as cowboy boots, she would have heard if there was something off about him.

"You're really doing this," she said aloud in her car. She'd made up her mind to take a huge leap of faith with Jerod. She'd tried love before and had been devastated when it hadn't worked out.

Now she was ready to try a marriage completely without love. She could honor Jerod as her husband without any messy emotions getting involved. The only thing that gave her pause was the fact that at some point they would have to have a physical interaction for her to get pregnant.

However, she'd always wanted more than one child. In fact, she'd always wanted a big family, but she'd given up that dream, among others, when Cody had left her.

A shiver raced up her back. Although she had never had a one-night stand in her life, she figured having sex with Jerod would be like a series of one-night stands in order to achieve the ultimate goal of getting pregnant.

She was pleased that he was willing to give her a little wedding rather than just going to the justice of the peace. Since this would be the one and only time she would marry, she wanted it to be a nice ceremony, although she wasn't expecting a lot. She had no family to invite, as her mother was dead and she hadn't spoken to her father since she'd moved to Bitterroot. But she did have some friends and coworkers she'd like to invite.

My God, if they really went through with this, then in ten days she would be a married woman. If she wanted everyone to believe the marriage was real, there were people she was going to have to lie to. She deeply regretted that one of those people was her son.

She didn't intend to say anything to anyone until she was absolutely certain the wedding was on. She'd wait for a phone call from Jerod the next day to see if he was actually following through on the wedding arrangements. She'd wait to see if he was the one who changed his mind about the whole thing. She'd wait to see if ultimately she was the one who would chicken out of the whole thing.

Krista had agreed to watch Caleb for her while she went to talk to Jerod, and she now headed to her friend's house to pick up her son. They often babysat for each other, and it worked out great since the two boys were best friends.

As close as she and Krista were as friends, Krista was just another person she'd have to lie to. She didn't even want her very best friend to know the truth about the marriage. She would be too embarrassed to tell anyone that this wasn't a union born of love, but rather of need and desires that had nothing to do with love.

The sun had begun to sink in the western sky, and this evening those skies were painted in beautiful pinks and oranges. The beauty felt like a promise, not just of a new day coming after the darkness of night, but of a new life for her.

However, she had a feeling this marriage wouldn't change things too much in her day-to-day existence. The only real difference would be that the man who was working as a ranch hand on her ranch would also be sleeping in her bed each night. It would be awkward at first, but eventually, hopefully they would grow more comfortable with each other.

She shoved all these thoughts out of her mind as she approached the turn for Krista's house.

Krista lived just off Main Street in an older two-story house with a nice wraparound porch. When Lily pulled up in the driveway, Krista was enveloped in a bright blue blanket and seated in a porch chair, and the two boys were in the front yard throwing a football back and forth.

"Ah, Mom," Caleb said with a groan when she got out of her car. "We just came out to play ball."

"You have fifteen minutes or so, and then we need to head home," she said and then joined Krista on her porch. She sank down in the porch chair facing her friend. "You look all cozy," she said to Krista.

"Nothing like a soft, snuggly blanket on a crisp fall evening," Krista replied. She raised one of her perfectly arched blond brows. "You were pretty closemouthed when you ask me to watch Caleb for you. Are you going to tell me where you've been?"

"No. It's a secret," Lily said and forced a laugh. "Maybe I'll tell you in another few days or so."

Krista sat up taller in the chair. "Oh, now you have me really intrigued. Does this have anything to do with Brad Walsh?"

"Good Lord, no," Lily replied. Brad Walsh was a fellow teacher, and he'd been after Lily for the past year to go out with him. He was like a bad penny who seemed to show up wherever she went in public.

"That man definitely has the hots for you,"

Krista said with a laugh. "I was just wondering if you'd finally succumbed to his charm."

"What charm?" Lily replied. "I find Brad to be an overbearing jerk and a little bit creepy. I've tried to make him understand I'm not interested in dating him."

"He's definitely a man who doesn't take no for an answer when it comes to you." Krista pulled the blanket up closer around her neck.

"So, was Caleb good for you?" Lily asked in an effort to change the subject. Krista knew that Lily had been having some problems with Caleb lately.

"He was a perfect angel," Krista replied. "But you know he's always good for me. The two boys just get along so well together."

"It's so nice that they seem to like each other as much as we like each other," Lily said.

"The best doctor appointment I ever had was when I was six months pregnant and I met you," Krista said with a smile.

Lily laughed. "And I was almost nine months pregnant, and it was a great day for me, too."

Krista was a Bitterroot native, but Lily had moved here almost eleven years ago when her mother had been killed in a car accident and Lily had come into a small inheritance. At that time she'd been working as a traveling medical equipment salesperson and had driven through Bitterroot several times. The small town with its rich pastureland and picturesque Main Street had charmed her. She'd made the move here, met Cody and the rest was history.

The two friends visited for a little while longer about school-related stuff, and then Lily rose. "I've got to get moving. Caleb needs a bath before bedtime, and I still have some papers to grade before tomorrow."

"Ugh, don't remind me. I've got a stack inside waiting for me to grade," Krista replied. "I'd rather just get in my car and take a little ride to destress me."

Lily laughed. "You and your little rides. I've never understood how being behind the wheel of the car destresses you."

"It's just the way I usually sort out my thoughts," Krista replied. She got up from her seat, as well. "I'm just glad that sometimes you take those little rides with me."

Lily laughed. "All in the name of friendship. Caleb, say good-night to Henry. It's time for us to go," Lily said. "Krista, I'll see you in the morning."

Two hours later Lily stepped out of her shower and pulled her nightshirt over her head. As she crawled in beneath the sheets, a new shiver raced up her spine.

If all went as planned, then in ten days she would get married, and that night she would be in this bed with Jerod Steen. Her shiver wasn't because she found the idea totally repugnant— rather, as she thought of his broad shoulders and muscled chest naked and against her own, a wave of sweet heat rushed through her and caused the shiver.

It had been almost ten years since she'd been held in a man's arms, ten years since she'd felt a man's touch on her body. At least she found Jerod physically attractive. But what if he didn't find her so? She knew she wasn't a raving beauty.

Boring Lil, that's how she always thought of herself. She had boring brown hair, and while her eyes were blue, they weren't a pretty crystal blue like Krista's.

Boring Lil, that's the way Krista had always made her feel. Krista was cute and sassy and the life of any party, while Lily usually stood in a corner and watched other people having fun. More than anything, lately she'd just thought of herself as a total loser.

For the past four years since Krista's husband had divorced her, she had been going hard-core to find another husband, while that had been the last thing Lily had been looking for. And yet it was Lily who would be getting married in ten days. Strange how life worked out. That was her last conscious thought before she fell asleep.

* * *

Jerod walked toward the big white two-story house in the distance. He'd eaten his lunch quickly and now intended to take the rest of his lunch time to talk to Cassie.

He hated that he was going to lie to his boss. He hated that he had to lie to anyone, but he intended to honor Lily's request that nobody know the truth about their relationship or lack thereof. He also needed to tell Cassie that starting the day after the wedding, he'd be working on Lily's place and would no longer be living or working on the Holiday spread.

When he reached the house, he knocked on the back door. Cassie opened the door and greeted him with a smile. Cassie was a petite blonde with bright blue eyes. She was cute, but had a will of steel. "Jerod, come on in. I was just making lunch for Dillon."

Dillon Bowie was not only Cassie's husband, he was also the chief of police for the town of Bitterroot. "Dillon," Jerod said to the dark-haired man who sat at the table.

"Don't tell me you're here to report trouble," Dillon said. "Things have been fairly quiet around here lately, and I'm hoping they stay that way."

Jerod laughed. "Don't worry, I'm not here about any kind of trouble. I am here to ask Cassie a big favor."

"Well, sit down and ask," Cassie said. She set a plate with a sandwich and chips in front of Dillon. "Jerod, have you eaten lunch?"

"Yeah, I already ate with the men." Jerod sat across from Dillon, and a case of nerves suddenly raced through his veins. Cassie sat next to him and looked at him expectantly.

Jerod cleared his throat. "I...uh...want to get married a week from this Saturday, and I was wondering if I...we could...uh...have the wedding in your barn?"

She stared at him for a long moment, and then a wide smile curved her lips and her bright blue eyes twinkled with excitement. "Oh, Jerod, I'm so happy for you. Who is the lucky bride?"

"Lily Kidwell," he replied.

"Oh, I've worked with her on a number of charity events. She's a lovely woman." Cassie replied. "Of course you can have the wedding in the barn. A week from Saturday? That's awfully quickly. Who is your wedding planner?"

Jerod stared at her blankly. "Wedding planner? Uh... I guess that's me. I told Lily to buy her dress and I'd take care of everything else."

"Have you ordered flowers or talked to the bakery about a cake?"

"Not yet." Jerod frowned. What all was involved in planning a wedding? He really had no idea. They'd only just started talking about it, and he already felt as if he were in way over his head. Flowers...a cake...he hadn't even thought about those things.

"So, basically what you're really saying is that you don't have a clue and need a planner." Cassie's smile widened. "Well, now you have one. I'll take care of things. I think I might know what a woman wants for her wedding better than you."

Dillon groaned. "Let me warn you, Jerod. When my wife gets hold of something, she's like a dog with a toy. She'll shake it until all the stuffing falls out."

Cassie slapped her husband affectionately on his shoulder and then looked back at Jerod. "So, what have you already done?"

"Uh...nothing," Jerod confessed. "To be honest, I'm really not sure where to begin. But as of right now, I haven't done anything. I figured I needed to make sure it was okay with you to use the barn before I lined up anything else."

"What time do you plan to have the ceremony?" Cassie asked.

"I don't know...maybe ten in the morning," Jerod said tentatively.

"We'll have it at three in the afternoon with a reception to follow," Cassie replied.

"See what I mean?" Dillon said with a teasing smile at his wife. "She won't be happy until she has everything her way."

"He obviously needs help, and I just want to help," Cassie replied and then frowned. "It's going to be tough to pull everything together in such a short time, but we can do it." She clapped her hands together. "I'm so excited. I want you and Lily to have a wedding to remember."

"Cassie, I didn't mean for you to take all this on," he protested.

Dillon shook his head and laughed. "Trust me, Jerod. She isn't doing you a favor. You're doing her a favor by letting her do this." He smiled affectionately at his wife. "She's needed a project, and you just handed her one."

"Well, I really do appreciate it," Jerod replied and stood. "I'll be glad to pay you for all your work, Cassie."

"Nonsense," she replied. "It's my pleasure to do this."

"You keep track of all the expenses, and I'll pay you for everything."

"I'll let you know how the plans are going. Expect a lot of phone calls from me." Cassie also rose from the table. "Now get out of here so I can get busy. The only thing you need to do is decide who you want to officiate over the ceremony and set things up with him or her."

"I can do that. Let me know if there's anything else you need me to take care of." He shifted from one foot to the other. "There's one more thing.

After the wedding, I won't be working or living here anymore. Lily has a big spread, and that's where I'll be working. I'm sorry, Cassie."

"Don't be sorry, Jerod. Of course I really hate to lose you, but my aunt Cass's ultimate goal for all you cowboys was that eventually you'd find love and be happy," Cassie replied. "You've been a good and reliable ranch hand for me, Jerod. And now it's time you are a good ranch hand for your own family."

An unexpected surge of grief followed Jerod as he left the house and headed back to the cowboy dining room. It felt like the end of an era. Big Cass was gone, and now he was leaving the only home and the men he had known for years.

The grief was quickly swallowed up by excitement. He was eager to sit down with Lily and look at the books of the ranch. He was hoping to identify why it wasn't more productive and make it prosperous. He was also elated that hopefully in the future Lily would give him his dream of a family of his own. This was the beginning of a new life for him, and he was eager for it to begin.

But it wouldn't happen if Lily had changed her mind overnight. As he worked throughout the afternoon, that was the biggest question in his head. When he spoke to her later this evening, would she tell him she'd changed her mind and no longer wanted the marriage?

Now that Cassie had taken over the planning, he hoped Lily was still all in for this to happen. He'd already spoken to Dusty and Mac, who had sworn their silence in how this marriage had come about.

After he'd eaten dinner, instead of moving to the rec part of the dining area, he went back to his own room. He sank down on the edge of the bed with his phone in his hand. Very little made Jerod nervous. He could face down a stubborn cow or a coyote causing trouble. He could tangle with an enraged bull or control a misbehaving horse, but calling Lily had him sweating with nerves.

He finally got up the nerve and punched in her number. She answered on the first ring. "Hi, Jerod."

"Hey, Lily. How are you doing today?"

"Okay, what about you?"

"I'm fine. Uh… I was just wondering if you'd had time to think about what we talked about yesterday. I was…uh…wondering if maybe you've changed your mind about things?" He held his breath.

"I haven't… I mean, I've thought about it and I haven't changed my mind. Have you?"

"No, not at all," he replied hurriedly. "In fact, I spoke to Cassie this afternoon, and she's not only agreed to let us get married in the barn, but she's going to act as a sort of wedding planner and get it all organized for us."

"Wow, that's really nice of her."

"Have you talked to Caleb about any of this yet?" he asked. He thought of the young boy who looked a lot like his mother with his brown hair and blue eyes.

"Not yet. I wanted to make certain you weren't going to change your mind. I'll have a conversation with him tonight and let him know what's happening."

"Lily, I'm definitely not going to change my mind. A week from this Saturday, I'm planning on marrying you if you'll have me. In fact, Cassie is planning for a three o'clock ceremony. Does that work for you?"

"That sounds fine." She released a small laugh. "My social calendar is pretty open for that day."

"And I was wondering if maybe you would let me take you and Caleb out to dinner tomorrow night at the café. It would be our first official outing together as a couple." Once again he found himself holding his breath in anticipation.

"I won't lie to you, the very idea of going out in public and testing if people believe we've been dating makes me nervous. But, if we're going to keep our…uh…business arrangement a secret, then I guess it's important we be seen out together from now on so people will believe we're a couple. So, yes, we'd love to have dinner with you tomorrow."

"Great, then how about I pick you two up around five thirty tomorrow evening?"

"We'll be ready."

The two said their goodbyes, and he hung up. As he stood from the edge of his bed, a wave of relief shot through him. It looked like everything was a go. In less than two weeks, he'd be a married man and building a new future for himself and Lily.

Although it wasn't a traditional happily-ever-after, he was hoping it would be a happily-ever-after nevertheless, and there was nothing he could foresee that would mess that up for them.

Chapter 3

At five fifteen the next afternoon, Lily looked in the bathroom mirror one last time. Her hair was neat and her makeup had been carefully applied. She wore a pair of jeans and a coral sweater that coworkers had told her was a good color for her.

She'd had a talk with Caleb the night before and had told him that she'd been dating Jerod and they were planning to be married. To say he'd been shocked was an understatement. She'd asked him if he had any questions and how he felt about it, but he'd grown quiet and hadn't talked to her about any of his feelings.

She hoped Caleb would be good at dinner tonight and that he didn't have an angry outburst. She hated it when her son refused to speak to her about important things, and she considered her getting married to Jerod definitely an important thing in his life.

Leaving the bathroom, she couldn't help the nervous energy that raced through her. She hadn't been on a date for over a decade. At least over dinner maybe she would learn more about the man she was going to marry.

Caleb sat in the living room watching a television show. "All ready to go?" she asked.

He shrugged. "I guess."

"Are you hungry?" She sank down next to him on the sofa.

"A little."

"Before Jerod arrives, is there anything you want to talk to me about?"

"No, I'm good," he replied.

"You've always told me you thought that Jerod was pretty cool when you've spent time with him at the community center."

"Yeah, but I didn't know he was going to be my new stepdad," Caleb replied.

At that moment she heard the crunch of gravel outside, indicating the arrival of Jerod. Her nerves jangled as she stood and waited for his knock on the door. When the knock came, she grabbed her jacket from the hall closet and tossed Caleb his jacket. She then opened the door and greeted Jerod.

He wore a pair of jeans and a long-sleeved navy blue turtleneck. She had forgotten how handsome he was. "Hi, Lily." He greeted her with a tentative smile.

"Hi, Jerod. We're ready to go."

Minutes later she was in the passenger seat of the king-cab pickup, Caleb was in the back seat and they were heading into town. She was acutely aware of Jerod's presence next to her. He smelled of minty shaving cream and a fresh-scented cologne that was very pleasing.

"How was your day?" he asked, breaking the slightly uncomfortable silence that had begun to build between them.

"It was good. How was yours?"

"It was fine." He looked in his rearview mirror. "What about you, Caleb? Did you have a good day?"

"It was okay," he replied in a half mumble.

Lily appreciated him trying to bring Caleb into their conversation, but her son obviously wasn't much interested.

"It was a pretty day today," Jerod said.

"It was nice. I've always loved fall," she replied.

He flashed her a quick smile. "Me, too. It's my favorite of the seasons."

She and Jerod continued with small talk until they arrived at the café.

It was Thursday night, and the place was packed as usual, causing a new jangle of nerves inside her. There were so many people here, and it felt like a baptism by fire to test the believability of their "relationship."

"Okay?" Jerod asked her as they got out of the truck.

She flashed him a shaky smile. "I'm fine," she said with more confidence than she felt.

The three of them walked inside the front door, and immediately Lily felt as if a hundred eyes were upon them.

There was a long counter where singles could sit on stools to eat. The rest of the space inside was relegated to booths around the sides and tables and chairs in the center.

The interior was painted a cheerful yellow with pictures of mouth-watering food on the walls. Normally she found it a pleasant place, but tonight she felt as if she was on display.

Jerod led them to an empty booth toward the back, and it was only when they were seated that she began to relax a bit.

Jerod sat across from her, and Caleb slid in next to her. Immediately waitress Julia Hatfield stopped to offer them menus and get their drink orders.

When she had the drink orders, Julia scurried away from the booth, and Lily and Caleb opened the menus. "Aren't you going to look at the menu?" she asked Jerod.

"I've eaten here often enough I have the whole thing memorized," he replied.

"Mom and I almost never get to eat out," Caleb said.

"Then we'll have to change that once your mother and I get married," Jerod replied.

"Just because you're marrying my mom doesn't mean that you are going to be my dad," Caleb replied with a frown and a belligerent edge to his voice.

Before Lily could say another word, Jerod smiled at Caleb. "Well, of course not," he said easily. "I would never try to replace your father, Caleb. However, I'd like to eventually become somebody you like and somebody you can trust. We've always gotten along well at the community center."

Caleb grunted and then closed his menu. "I just want a cheeseburger and some cheese fries."

"Well, I'm planning on getting a big steak with a baked potato," Jerod said.

"And I'm leaning toward the special of a stuffed pepper," Lily said.

"Yuck," Caleb exclaimed, making both Jerod and Lily laugh. The shared laughter immediately put Lily more at ease. As they waited for their meals to arrive, they talked about likes and dislikes of food.

"There's really not much I don't like, although I'm not fond of sloppy joes," Jerod said.

"What's wrong with them?" Caleb asked. "I think they're awesome."

"I've only had them prepared by Cookie, the cook at the ranch, and he puts something in them that kind of turns my stomach," Jerod explained.

"Well, you need to taste Mom's sloppy joes. She makes awesome ones," Caleb replied. "She's a really good cook."

"So at least I know I won't starve to death once we get married," Jerod said teasingly. The more he said it, the more comfortable she got with the idea of the marriage. Still, the whole thing felt a bit surreal. Lily should have many more doubts. Maybe she should have taken more time to think this through. But she didn't have time. Foreclosure was a real and imminent disaster, and Jerod was the fix for that.

"So, Lily, did you always want to be a teacher?" he asked.

"No, what I really wanted to be was a full-time rancher. When I moved here from Oklahoma City, that's what I intended, but things didn't exactly turn out well, and thankfully I had a teaching degree to fall back on. What about you? Have you always wanted to work on a ranch?"

"When I arrived at the Holiday Ranch when I was fifteen years old, I hadn't really given much thought to what I wanted to do with my life. All I knew at that time was learning to be a real cowboy was what was expected of me. Now I can't imagine doing anything else."

She knew the story of Cass's cowboys—the twelve runaway boys who were brought to the Holiday Ranch to get them off the streets and living a productive life. She had no idea what Jerod's life had been like for the first fifteen years, but she hoped someday he would share that with her.

"I want to be a real cowboy when I grow up," Caleb said. "Mom said I could work on our ranch and then when I got old enough she'd turn it over to me."

"That's great. Maybe I could teach you some things about being a real cowboy," Jerod said.

"Nah, that's okay," Caleb replied. "Just because you're marrying my mom doesn't mean you get to tell me what to do."

"Caleb," Lily said sharply. She would have reprimanded Caleb more for his rudeness if they had been at home, but she didn't want to get Caleb stirred up to the point where he'd make a scene in the café.

Thankfully, at that time their meals arrived.

"What I'm really hoping for is that we can get the ranch at a place where you could quit your teaching job and be a working partner with me," Jerod said once they'd been served and Julia had left their booth.

"That would be absolutely wonderful," she replied. "But I think it's going to take nothing short of a miracle to get to that place."

"I'm eager to sit down with you and Rod and look everything over," he replied.

"Rod and I will be ready whenever you are," she replied.

"I think Rod likes Mom," Caleb said, making Lily gasp.

"Why do you think that?" Jerod asked.

"I've seen him when he's getting ready to go into the house to talk to her and he always combs his hair and sprays that stuff in his mouth to make his breath smell good," Caleb replied.

"You never told me that before," Lily said in surprise. She had never, ever looked at Rod as a potential suitor. He was just a ranch hand that she depended on.

"Well, I guess he won't be combing his hair or having sweet breath after next week," Jerod said wryly. "He'll know your mother is a married lady."

"I'm just glad you aren't marrying creepy Mr. Walsh," Caleb said.

"And who is creepy Mr. Walsh?" Jerod asked.

"He's a fifth-grade teacher at the school," Lily explained.

"And he keeps asking Mom to go on dates with him, but she always tells him no. Sometimes I think he stalks her," Caleb added.

"What do you know about stalking?" Lily asked her son.

"I know a lot about it. I watched a movie where a woman was being stalked by an ex-boyfriend and then he wanted to kill her."

"Maybe I need to better monitor what you're watching on television, but now I intend to eat before my food gets cold," she said.

For the next few minutes they fell silent as they began to eat. Caleb had made it sound like all the men in Bitterroot were after Lily, and nothing could be further from the truth. Other than Brad hovering around her, no man had ever shown an interest in her. Not that she'd cared. She hadn't been interested in dating.

Before Cody had left her, he'd made it clear that she'd never be enough to keep a man happy. She wasn't pretty enough or lively enough to keep a man happy.

As far as Rod was concerned, she just assumed his combing his hair or whatever he did before he spoke to her was simply a matter of respect and not any romantic interest.

"So, what else do you two enjoy doing when you have spare time?" Jerod asked.

"I like to play catch with my best friend and play my video games," Caleb said.

"And when I get a few minutes to myself, I like to read, and I love to ride my horse. Boring, right?" she said.

"Not boring at all," he protested with a small laugh.

"I wish I had a horse," Caleb said. "How can I be a cowboy and not have a horse? I've been asking for one for forever."

"Eventually we'll see about a horse for you," Lily said, and then turned back to Jerod. "What about you? What do you like to do in your spare time?" she asked. She felt as if they were trying to catch up on months of dating in one dinner.

"I like listening to music, so most evenings Mac McBride plays his guitar and sings, and it's a nice way to relax," he replied.

"Will you miss that when you move into our place? I could get a guitar and maybe learn how to strum, but I can't do anything about my less-than-stellar singing voice," she said.

He laughed again. "Thank God you have a sense of humor."

She grinned at him. "I have a feeling we're both going to need one as all this unfolds." She held his gaze for a moment and then looked down at her plate. This time with him had been easy, but it had also been extremely superficial. She still didn't really know him, and he didn't really know her.

"Well, well, what have we here?" Brad Walsh appeared at the side of their booth.

"Hello, Brad," she said. "Do you know Jerod Steen? Jerod, this is Brad Walsh, one of my fellow teachers." Jerod half rose and offered his hand out for a shake.

Brad ignored Jerod's hand and instead focused on Lily. "I'm confused, Lily. I thought you told me you didn't date."

"I guess she was just waiting for the right man to come along," Jerod said as he sat back down again.

"Yeah, and they're getting married," Caleb added.

Brad looked stricken. "Is that true?"

"We're tying the knot a week from this Saturday," Jerod said. He smiled at Lily. "I finally talked her into being my bride."

Lily laughed. "He didn't have to talk too hard for me to agree."

"Then I guess congratulations are in order," Brad replied. "You sure have been closemouthed about all this."

"I am a rather private person," Lily said, slightly uncomfortable beneath Brad's intense gaze.

"Once again, congratulations to you both."

With a curt nod to Jerod, Brad left the side of their booth.

"So, that was creepy Mr. Walsh?" Jerod asked Caleb.

"Yeah. Next year he'll be my teacher, and nobody likes being in his class," Caleb replied. "He's really strict and mean."

By that time they had finished the meal, and once Jerod had paid, they left the café and got back in his truck. "You realize by this time tomorrow everyone in town will know we're getting married," she said. "Brad is not only slightly creepy, he's also a huge gossip," Lily said. "And in any case, half the town saw us out together tonight."

"That's okay by me," Jerod said. "Sooner or later everyone is going to know. It might as well be sooner. By the way, Cassie asked me today how many people we expect to come to the wedding. I don't have any family to invite, but I would like my friends at the ranch to be invited. What about you?"

"No family for me, either. I'd like to invite all the teachers and staff from the school. So, that would be about twenty. Is that too many?" she asked worriedly.

"No, I'm sure that's fine, and if you think of any more people you want there, just let me know.

I suppose at this point we only have time to invite people either by mouth or by email."

They talked about the invites for a few more minutes, and by that time they were back at her place. "Caleb, go get into the shower," she said as the three of them stepped inside the house.

As Caleb disappeared into the bathroom, Lily turned to Jerod. "Would you like a cup of coffee or something?"

"No, I'm good," he replied. "I know you have school tomorrow, so I'll just head on home."

"Thank you so much for dinner," she replied.

The two of them walked out the front door and onto her porch. The few times Jerod had been out to talk to her about Caleb, they had those conversations out here. She'd sit in the porch swing and he'd sit in the porch chair opposite her.

Now he stood closer to her than he normally did, and his nearness made her heart beat just a little faster. "I enjoyed having dinner with you," he said and took another step closer.

"I enjoyed it, too," she replied.

"We'll do it again in the next couple of days," he replied. He leaned toward her, and for a moment she wondered if he was going to kiss her. She was surprised to realize she wouldn't mind a simple, quick kiss.

He reached out and swept a strand of her hair away from her face and then stepped back from her. "I'll call you sometime tomorrow. Good night, Lily."

She murmured a good night and then watched as he walked back to his truck, got in and drove away. In just a little over a week, the man would be her husband.

For the first time since she'd agreed to this crazy plan, new doubts raced through her mind. Was this really what she wanted to do? Give herself to a man in marriage in exchange for him saving her ranch? It sounded so rash...so desperate.

Sure, they had just enjoyed a pleasant dinner together, but she still didn't really know him. Tonight had been easy, but it hadn't done much to reveal who they really were to each other.

Was he a sex addict? Another kind of addict? Did he have any inner demons that would rear their heads once they were married? Although she'd never heard anything bad about Jerod, who was he behind closed doors?

She closed and locked her front door. Only time would tell, but she had to admit that she was a bit afraid of what she might be getting herself and her son into.

The wedding day dawned with bright sunshine and unusually warm temperatures. Lily had found a beautiful wedding dress in a shop on Main Street and it, her shoes and her makeup bag were now packed and in her truck to head to Cassie's home.

Cassie had insisted she come to the house and dress there, and Caleb had been picked up by Krista earlier that day. Krista had been utterly shocked to hear that Lily was getting married. She'd been with Lily when she'd bought her dress, and she'd offered to have Caleb come to the wedding with her and Henry and then he would spend the night with her. Lily had appreciated her best friend's support.

Lily had no idea what the Holiday Ranch barn looked like or what arrangements had been made there for a wedding. The only thing she did know for sure was that Jerod had gotten John Tenent, the Methodist Church minister, to officiate at the ceremony.

As Lily got into her truck to head to Cassie's, her nerves screamed in her veins. These last ten days had flown by with scarcely time to think. Was she insane to be going through with this? Was this the right thing to do, or would it be the biggest mistake she'd ever made?

She'd already made one mistake in her life, and that was falling in love with and trusting a cowboy who had disappeared from her life the minute she'd told him she was pregnant.

At least she didn't love Jerod. This was more of a business transaction than anything. She didn't have to worry about Jerod hurting her heart, because her heart wasn't at all involved. And if he even thought of physically or emotionally abusing her or Caleb, he would be out of the house and divorced so fast his head would spin.

She pulled up in the back of Cassie and Dillon's house and parked, her heart beating a million miles a minute. In two hours' time, she would become Mrs. Jerod Steen.

Cassie flew out of the back door, a blond-haired, blue-eyed whirlwind of energy and excitement. "I'm so glad you're here." She gave Lily a big hug and then released her. "We'll get you set up in a bedroom where you can dress, and if you want, I'll help you with your hair and makeup."

"Oh, you don't need to do that," Lily protested. "You've already done more than enough for me."

"Nonsense. Half the fun of your wedding day is having somebody flutter and fuss over you. Come on, I'll help you carry your things in."

For the next two hours, Lily was pampered and primped over by Cassie, and all the while she told Lily what a great guy she was marrying. "Jerod is patient and steady," Cassie said. "I'm so happy you two found each other." She continued to extoll Jerod's virtues as she helped fix Lily's hair.

Before Cassie started working on Lily's makeup, she brought her a glass of champagne to sip. "I feel like I'm a princess," Lily said.

"Good, that's the way you should feel on this special day," Cassie replied.

When it was finally almost time for the wedding, Cassie changed into a pretty, short pink dress and then helped Lily into her wedding gown.

When she was finished, she stepped back from Lily and clapped her hands together. "Oh, Lily, you look absolutely beautiful." She twirled Lily around to give her a view of herself in a full-length mirror.

Lily's breath caught in her throat as she stared at her own reflection. Despite her financial situation, she'd splurged a little bit on the dress. It was a long column of white silk with the bodice decorated with tiny sequins and beading.

Despite the fact that she was hardly a virgin, she'd given herself permission to wear the beautiful white dress, knowing it would be the one and only wedding she would ever have.

Cassie had done magic with Lily's hair, weaving a band of tiny beads through it. She'd also done Lily's makeup, making Lily feel prettier than she'd ever felt in her entire life.

"It's time, Lily," Cassie said. "Dillon is waiting to drive us down to the barn."

The nerves that had been relatively quiet for the past hour burst into life once again, racing her heartbeat and twisting her stomach. It was time for her to marry Jerod. Even though they had gone out to eat together several more times in the past week, he was still a virtual stranger to her. With Caleb in attendance each time they had been together, their conversations had remained light and without any real depth.

Dillon awaited them at the back door, looking handsome in a black suit. "Your chariot awaits," he said. He ushered them outside, where a white town car was parked.

He helped Lily into the back seat and then helped Cassie into the seat next to Lily. Lily reached out and grasped Cassie's hand. "I'll never be able to thank you for what you've done for me."

Cassie squeezed her hand. "You have no idea what you've done for me. I've had such fun planning this, and in any case, I had a lot of help from other people in town."

For the first time, Lily noticed all the cars parked along the drive and down by the barn. Wedding guests were apparently all in place. Dillon parked in front of the closed barn doors. He opened the door for Lily and helped her out and then went around and helped Cassie from the car.

"Lily, I know you don't have a father here, so I thought I'd lend you my husband to walk you down the aisle. Does that work with you?" Cassie asked. Tears burned at Lily's eyes. "Lily Kidwell, don't you dare cry. I worked on putting on the perfect eye makeup for you, and if you cry it all off now I'm going to be mad."

"And trust me, you don't want to see her mad," Dillon said softly, making Lily and Cassie laugh.

"I'm going to sneak on in." Cassie looked at her husband. "You know what to do." With these words she disappeared into the barn and left the door partway open.

"You doing okay?" Dillion asked as he took Lily's arm in his.

She nodded, her emotions still so close to the surface she was afraid to speak for fear of crying. A moment later a guitar began playing the wedding march, and the barn doors opened.

Her breath caught in her throat as she saw the barn's interior. It had truly been transformed into a beautiful venue, with chairs on either side of an aisle that was lined by huge vases of flowers and flickering little lights. It was like walking into a magical garden with hundreds of lightning bugs.

Jerod and John Tenent stood at the end of the aisle. Clad in a black tuxedo with a white shirt and black tie, Jerod looked somber and incredibly handsome. Her heart quickened. This good-looking man who looked at her so intently was about to become her husband. As she approached him, a small smile curved his lips, making him look less stern.

When she reached him, Dillon released her arm

and took a seat next to Cassie. And then it was just her and Jerod and the minister, who indicated they should hold hands. His hands were warm and slightly callused and felt incredibly strong and capable.

Everything that happened next went by in a dreamlike haze. They repeated vows, and he slid a pretty ring on her finger, and then John indicated Jerod could kiss his bride.

"May I?" Jerod whispered to her.

She nodded, and then Jerod's lips were on hers. His lips were warm and more than pleasing even though the kiss was short. The crowd cheered as Jerod grabbed her hand and they walked back down the aisle as husband and wife.

He led her out of the barn. "We're to wait out here until Cassie comes out to get us," he said.

"Okay." She suddenly felt unaccountably shy. She didn't know what to say or how to act around the man who was now her husband. Everything felt so unreal.

"Lily, are you all right?" he asked softly.

"I'm fine. To be honest, I think maybe I'm just a little overwhelmed at the moment. I can't believe what Cassie did to make everything so beautiful."

"And it's not over yet. Cookie has been busy all day making food for the reception, and Cassie hired the Croakin' Frog band to play music for dancing."

"We need to figure out something nice we can do for her," Lily replied.

"Definitely," he said. "We'll put our heads together and come up with something. By the way, you look absolutely lovely."

She felt the warmth that leaped into her cheeks at his compliment. "Thank you. And you look very handsome."

"Thanks."

For several minutes a silence grew between them. "This feels a little surreal," she finally said.

He offered her a smile. "It does, doesn't it? I know things are kind of awkward between us now, but I'm hoping it will get easier with time. By the way, Caleb looked quite handsome in his suit."

Lily laughed. "You have no idea how hard I had to fight with him to wear it. If he'd had his way, he would have worn a pair of jeans and a T-shirt."

Jerod reached up and tugged at his black tie. "I understand his feelings," he said with a laugh.

For the next few minutes they small-talked about some of the guests in attendance. "I saw your friend the creepy Mr. Walsh here."

She winced. "I couldn't exactly invite all the other teachers and not invite him."

"That's okay. I don't have a problem with him as long as he respects our marriage."

"The only person I've had a problem with is Krista, who refused to speak to me for two days for not telling her that we had been dating and were getting married. But she got over it." She released a small laugh. "Krista can never stay mad at me for long. We're very best friends."

"That's the way I feel about Mac McBride. Even though I'm close to all the other cowboys I grew up with, I've always been closest to Mac."

"He seems like a nice man," she replied.

"He is. He's very laid-back and calm. Sometimes I think he's not only a horse whisperer, but also a people whisperer. He just naturally makes people calm down and chill out."

"That's a nice quality to have," she replied. But she was more interested in what qualities Jerod possessed, something any normal person would know before getting married.

At that moment Cassie opened the barn door and motioned the two of them inside. Once again the space had been transformed. Tables and chairs now lined the walls, leaving a large area in the center for dancing. A full buffet and bar were present, along with a head table to which Cassie led them among cheers and hoots from the guests.

Mac stood and held up his drink. Jerod and Lily picked up the champagne-filled glasses at their table. "A toast," Mac said. "To Jerod and Lily. May your futures be filled with love and laughter and a bunch of cattle and children."

Everyone laughed and drank. Cassie took pictures, and then the band began to play a slow country song and it was time for Jerod and Lily to have their first dance together. They took to the center of the dance floor, and Jerod pulled her into his arms.

Despite the crazy circumstances and her nervousness, his strong arms holding her felt wonderful. They moved slowly to the music, his body mere inches from hers. He smelled so good, and she fought the impulse to lean her head into the crook of his neck.

She wasn't ready to fall into bed with him, and she had no idea what he might expect from her tonight, but in this moment…in his arms…she felt safe and protected, and it felt so good after so many years of being all alone.

Their dance officially kicked off the party. Soon the dance floor was filled, and Lily found herself dancing with a number of people, as did Jerod. When she had a moment, she pulled Caleb up to dance with her. Even though he protested, when he saw Henry dancing with his mother, Caleb relaxed and danced with Lily.

They stopped dancing long enough to fill plates from the buffet. Cookie had prepared pulled pork and baked beans, potato and macaroni salads. There was also fresh fruit and a lettuce salad and several other dishes that were sure to feed and please the crowd.

After they ate, Cookie and Mac came in carrying a beautiful, three-tiered wedding cake. Once again tears burned at Lily's eyes. Cassie and the people of Bitterroot had truly given her the dream she'd once wanted…a wedding to remember.

Okay, so in her dreams of long ago she hadn't envisioned her making a business arrangement with the man she would marry. She hadn't envisioned her groom being a relative stranger, but none of that took away from the absolute beauty of her wedding.

After the cake cutting, Carol Jenkins, a fellow teacher and good friend, came up to her. "You lucky girl," she exclaimed. "I'd had my sights on Jerod for months, and you just quietly move in and scoop him up."

Lily laughed. "If you're waiting for me to apologize for taking Jerod off the dating market, I won't."

Carol pulled her into a hug. "I just hope you two are very happy. You deserve it."

"Thank you," Lily replied once Carol released her.

Many of the guests had already left when Lily and Jerod finally approached Dillon and Cassie to say good-night and give their thanks once again.

"I'll never be able to thank you for everything," Lily said to Cassie. "You really gave me a night I will never forget."

"You two deserve all the happiness in the world," Cassie replied.

Then Lily and Jerod got into his truck to head to her house with the understanding they would return the next day to pick up her truck.

Almost immediately after they left the Holiday Ranch, a new awkward silence grew between them. Nervous tension tightened Lily's chest as she thought of the night to come. Would he really expect to have sex with her tonight…so quickly?

Wouldn't most men anticipate sex on their wedding night? After all, he knew she'd made arrangements for Caleb not to be in the house tonight, leaving the two of them all alone.

"I can't wait to get out of these clothes and into something more comfortable," Jerod said, finally breaking the charged silence.

"I agree. I'm looking forward to putting my jogging pants on and just relaxing." If he thought she'd bought some slinky, sexy lingerie for the night, he was sadly mistaken. She would be wearing the same cotton nightshirt she always wore.

Once again a strained silence built between them as Lily contemplated the night to come. She wished she knew Jerod well enough to know what he was thinking, but she had no clue what might be going on inside his head.

"It was a nice ceremony," he said, breaking up the silence once again.

"I have to admit, the actual ceremony kind of went by in a haze for me," she replied.

"Having regrets?"

She hesitated a moment. "No regrets."

He flashed her a quick glance. "You took a moment before answering. You aren't going to back out on me, are you?"

"If I was going to back out on you, it would have been before I said, 'I do.' Are you going to back out on me?"

"What do you mean?" Again he gazed at her and then back at the road.

"Are you really going to go into the bank on Monday and clear up the missed mortgage payments?"

"Of course I'm going to do that. It was part of my promise to you," he replied.

"I've had a man promise me a lot of things before, but all those promises were broken," she replied.

"I'm not that man. I never break my promises, Lily," he replied. "And throughout this marriage, I hope to prove that to you over and over again."

Despite her nerves about the night to come, a warmth whispered through her at his words. Maybe eventually she would come to trust Jerod, but it was just too soon. And in any case, he'd just turned into the long drive that led to her house, and all she could think of was what would be expected of her when they were alone on their wedding night.

She'd left her porch light on before she'd left earlier in the day, and the moon overhead was full, pouring down illumination that painted her house in a silvery light.

She frowned. "What's that hanging from the porch railing?"

"I can't make it out from here, but it's white, so it's probably some sort of congratulation decoration."

He parked the truck, and together they got out. Jerod grabbed a duffel bag from the back seat and then they approached the porch. "It looks like it's a bride doll," Lily said. She took another step closer and then gasped.

It was indeed, a bride doll, but half of the hair was missing, the eyes had been gouged out and were leaking something that looked like blood, and a knife protruded from the chest. It was gory and horrifying and felt like a personal threat against her.

"Lily, let's go inside and I'll call Dillon," Jerod said.

With fingers that trembled, she unlocked the front door and they stepped inside. "Wait here," Jerod said to her. He then disappeared down the hallway, and she realized he was checking the house to make sure nobody was inside.

Lily sank down on the sofa. Dear God, what

was happening right now? Who would leave such a horrible thing for her? The few moments she had seen the doll, it had felt as if a malevolent energy was radiating from it…a malevolence directed at her.

Her biggest concern and question before now had been what Jerod would expect of her on her wedding night. Now her biggest fear was that there was somebody out there who hated her enough to leave the mutilated doll. What did it mean? A shiver of fear worked up her spine. It felt like a curse on their marriage.

And what might happen next? A new, icy shiver raced up her spine.

Chapter 4

Jerod sat next to Lily on the sofa to wait for Dillon to arrive. The grotesque doll concerned him, but he could tell it had scared the absolute hell out of Lily. Her features were strained, and her face was pale as her fingers worried a strand of her hair.

"I'm so sorry, Lily," he said. "It's a terrible way to end what had been a great day."

"I just… I just can't imagine who would do such a thing. Why somebody would leave that for me…for us to find."

"I sure don't know who would do something like this. The cowboys at the ranch always play jokes on each other, but they would never do something like this," he replied.

"It's a horrid, terrible thing."

"It is, and hopefully Dillon will be able to figure something out." He wanted to take her hand in
his to assure her she wasn't all alone in this. But
he was afraid she might not welcome his touch.

He'd intended that this night they would just
talk and relax and get to know each other better.
He certainly hadn't planned on anything sexual
happening with her so soon.

However right now his biggest concern was
Lily and the question of who might have left her
such a horrible effigy. "Do you think it's possible
that Brad Walsh left this for you?"

She dropped her hand from her hair and released a deep sigh. "He would be the first on my
short list of suspects. In fact, he's the only person
I can imagine doing something like this. But on
the other hand, I can't imagine him doing something so…so wicked."

She had looked so pretty walking down the
aisle, and he hated that this was happening, that
on their wedding night while she was still clad in
her beautiful bridal gown, they were waiting for
the chief of police to arrive.

He not only hated it for her, but he needed to
know if this was some kind of a threat against
her. She was now his wife, and he would protect
her with his life against any danger. He just didn't
know if the doll had been somebody's idea of a

sick joke or if it was meant as a very real threat against his new bride.

"Thank God Caleb isn't here," she said. "I would not want him to see or know about any of this."

"I agree. Children should never have to deal with adult issues."

"That's always been my philosophy," she replied. "Thank God Caleb didn't see this kind of ugliness."

At that moment there was a knock on the door. "That should be Dillon now." He got up and opened the door, and the lawman stepped inside. Jerod gestured Dillon to the chair, and then he returned to the sofa to sit next to Lily.

"I think I know why I'm here," Dillon said. "That doll is a nasty piece of work." He sat in the chair facing them. "Any idea who might be responsible for it? Lily, is there anyone you've been having trouble with lately?"

"Not really." She frowned. "Although I don't think Brad Walsh was overly happy that I was getting married. He's been asking me out for months, and I've always rejected him. But other than that, I can't think of anyone who would have any reason to do something like this."

"What about Caleb's father? Is he around at all?"

Her cheeks colored as if with embarrassment. "He hasn't been around since I told him I was pregnant with Caleb. I don't even know where he is right now or if he's even still alive."

"Jerod, what about you?"

Jerod looked at him in surprise. "What about me?"

"Is there anyone who might be upset that you got married?" Dillon asked.

He frowned thoughtfully. "Not that I can think of."

"Anyone you dated before you started dating Lily?" Dillon asked.

"I haven't done a whole lot of dating in the last few months. The only woman I was seeing before Lily was Donna Maddox, and that was only something casual." He felt embarrassed even to talk about his dating habits before Lily in front of her.

"Did she know it was just something casual?"

"I'm assuming she knew," Jerod replied. "We only went out a couple of times, and then we stopped seeing each other."

Dillon turned his attention back to Lily. "Is there anyone you were dating before Jerod who might feel betrayed by you getting married?"

"Nobody," she replied firmly. "I haven't dated anyone for the last ten years."

"What about at school? Any angry parents or staff who might have a grudge against you?"

Lily shook her head. "No, nobody."

"Was Brad still at the reception when you two left?" Dillon asked.

Jerod looked at Lily and then he looked back at Dillon. "I'm pretty sure he'd already left. Most of the guests were already gone by the time Lily and I left," he replied.

"That's what I thought," Dillion said with a frown. He rose from the chair. "Maybe somebody will get drunk tonight at the Watering Hole and brag about mutilating a bride doll. In the meantime, I'll do some investigating to try to find out who is responsible, and I'll take the doll with me."

"Good. I definitely want it gone," Lily said.

Jerod stood and walked with Dillon to the front door. "Lily, I'll be right back," Jerod said and then followed Dillon outside to his car, where Dillon grabbed a pair of gloves and an evidence bag big enough to hold the doll.

"I didn't want to say anything in front of Lily, but honestly even if I do find out who did this, there isn't much I can do about it. The most they could be charged with is possibly trespassing, and I can warn them to stay away from the property from now on."

"I'm just concerned about what the doll means in the long run," Jerod said as the two of them walked back to the porch. "Is it intended to be a threat to Lily?"

Dillon pulled on his plastic gloves. "I wish I could answer that, but I can't. Only time will tell us if this is just an isolated incident or not. If I was to guess, this is probably somebody's idea of a joke. Granted, it's a joke in bad taste."

"I would say so," Jerod replied drily.

The doll had been hung by a thick string around its neck. Dillon yanked on it and managed to get it off the overhead beam and into the evidence bag. "I seriously doubt if it's real blood on it. With Halloween right around the corner, there is lots of fake blood being sold in the stores, but I'll have it sent to the lab to see exactly what it is."

"Thanks, Dillon. We appreciate it," Jerod said.

Dillon gave him a rueful smile. "I'm sure this isn't exactly the way you anticipated this night ending."

"Not exactly," Jerod replied. "But I'm just hoping this doesn't completely ruin Lily's wedding day."

"I hope not, either," Dillon said. "Go back in to your bride. I'll be in touch over the next day or two."

The two men said good-night to each other, and then Jerod returned to the house. Lily remained on the sofa, her face still pale. "Is the doll gone?"

"It's gone. Are you okay?" he asked.

"I guess, although I still don't understand why somebody would leave that doll for me."

"Dillon thought it was quite possible it was somebody's idea of a very bad joke. Unfortunately we aren't going to get any answers about who left it tonight. Why don't we both get changed into more comfortable clothes?" he suggested. "Then maybe we can relax and talk for a little while before calling it a night."

"That sounds good to me," she replied. She got up from the sofa and headed for the master bedroom while he carried his duffel bag into the main bathroom to change his clothes. There was no reason to make her even more stressed out by going into her bedroom with her right now.

He took off the tux and carefully hung it on a hanger. He'd rented it from the local men's shop and would return it Monday when they went into town to deal with her bank issues.

He pulled on a pair of worn jeans and a T-shirt, combed his slightly shaggy hair and then carried his duffel bag back into the living room and sank back down on the sofa.

She joined him there minutes later. She was clad in a pair of gray jogging pants and a light pink T-shirt, but still a worried frown rode across her forehead.

"Lily, try not to worry about the bride doll too much," he said. "Maybe it really was just somebody's idea of a sick joke, or maybe it was Walsh expressing his displeasure with you, but no matter what it means, I would never let anyone harm you. I've definitely got your back."

The frown smoothed out a bit as she offered

him a small smile. "Thank you, that's good to know."

"I don't want that damned doll to define this day for you."

She raised her chin a notch, and her eyes flashed. "I refuse to let it."

An unexpected attraction kicked Jerod in the stomach. He'd never noticed before how truly beautiful her eyes were. They were a cornflower blue with unusually long lashes, and right now with them sparking with her anger, their beauty momentarily stole his breath away.

"It was a beautiful day," she continued. "It was like something out of a fairy tale for me and nothing like what I expected for a wedding pulled together so quickly."

He smiled. "Cassie definitely went above and beyond, but that doesn't really surprise me. As long as she's been at the ranch, she's shown us all many times what a kind, giving and caring woman she is."

"You were originally one of Big Cass's lost boys?" she asked and then grimaced. "I don't mean to be disrespectful or offensive, but that's a term I've heard used when referring to the cowboys at the Holiday Ranch."

"That's the way we always referred to ourselves, so no offense taken," he replied.

"How old were you when you came to the ranch?"

"I was fifteen. I was living on the streets in Oklahoma City and barely surviving when a social worker talked to me about going to Cass's ranch and working as a cowboy for her. All I knew at the time was Cass promised there would be a roof over my head and three meals a day to eat, and so I agreed to go."

He could tell Lily was relaxing as they talked, and that's exactly what he'd hoped would happen. This was also part of the getting to know each other on a slightly deeper level.

"So, why did you run away from home in the first place?" she asked. "If I'm prying, please just tell me."

He laughed. "Lily, I'm your husband. If anyone has a right to pry, it's you." He sobered, and his hand rose to touch the slightly raised scar on the side of his face. "I didn't really have a home to run away from. My mother was a raging alcoholic and drug addict, and most of the time we lived in a series of trashy motel rooms with a series of abusive and trashy men."

"Oh, Jerod. I'm so sorry."

He shrugged despite the old feelings of pain and betrayal that threatened to rise up. "It was a long time ago. Anyway, I just got tired of living the way we were, and I knew my mother wasn't going to change. I didn't want to stick around and watch her kill herself, so one night I packed my clothes and took off."

Once again he reached up and touched the scar that had ended his life with his mother. He wasn't ready to share the true horror of that night with Lily, or with anyone else. It was way too soon to trust her with all the pieces of his past.

He dropped his hand back to his lap. "Anyway, coming to the Holiday Ranch was the best thing that ever happened to me."

"How did you get the scar on your face?" she asked, apparently noticing him touching it.

"It was just a childhood accident," he replied. "Now it's your turn. Tell me about your parents." He needed to change the subject. He wasn't ready to tell her the truth about how he had received the scar. He needed to know and trust her more before he told her just how truly dysfunctional his life with his mother had been.

She frowned. "They divorced when I was six, and for the next twelve years I was the pawn they used to try to hurt each other. The divorce was quite acrimonious, and the issue of the custody of me was even worse. It was pretty miserable for me. I didn't feel like either of them really loved me. When I turned eighteen, I tried to maintain a relationship with them, but ultimately once I couldn't be used as a weapon between them anymore, they had very little interest in me and my life. And then, when I was twenty, my mother died in a car wreck."

"Oh, I'm so sorry, Lily," he replied.

She shrugged. "To be honest, when she died, I grieved for what had never been and the fact that I would never get a chance to have a real relationship with her. But she'd already been absent from my life for several years."

"Now, tell me about Caleb's father."

She sat up straighter. "There really isn't much to tell. His name was…is Cody Lee, and when I first met him he was working as a ranch hand for Abe Breckenridge." Abe was an older, well-respected rancher in the area.

"We had a whirlwind romance, and within months I was using an inheritance from my mother to buy this place with the understanding that Cody was going to marry me and work side by side with me to make this place a real success."

She looked down at her hands in her lap. "I was a complete fool. I trusted him and all the promises he made to me. I put him on my bank account and truly believed he loved me. But when I told him I was pregnant with his baby, he emptied my bank account and disappeared. I never saw or heard from him again." She gazed up at Jerod. "And that's my story." She shifted positions, moving close enough to him that he caught a whiff of a pleasant lilac scent wafting from her.

"It must have been rough, raising Caleb all alone and trying to keep this ranch up and running at the same time," he observed.

"It was difficult, and somehow I managed to screw up both things. The ranch is failing and Caleb is having temper fits I don't even understand. You know because we've talked about his temper before." For a moment she looked totally vulnerable and miserable.

He reached out and covered one of her hands with his. "Lily, I'm going to get this place running well, and maybe eventually Caleb will confide in us what is bothering him."

She turned her hand over and squeezed his. "That would be wonderful." She released a deep sigh and then pulled her hand from his.

"It's getting late. Maybe it's time for us to call it a night." The minute the words left his mouth, he felt a new tension radiating from her. And he had a feeling he knew exactly what had caused it. Was she really afraid he would insist on having sex with her tonight? They were still strangers to each other.

"Lily, I'm not expecting anything from you until we're both much more comfortable with each other, and you get to determine when that time might be. I would never force anything on you.

Even though we'll be sharing a bed, I promise you I'll try to stay on my own side."

Her relief appeared immediate. She instantly shot him a smile that not only curved her lips but also sparkled in her eyes. Once again he was struck by her loveliness. Why had he never noticed before?

"Thank you, Jerod. That means a lot to me, although I can't promise you that I'm not a bed hog. I've been sleeping alone for a lot of years, and I have no idea if I roll here and there or not."

He laughed. "I'll let you know in the morning if you hogged the bed." He stood and held out his hand to her. She took his hand, and he pulled her up off the sofa. He then grabbed his duffel and followed her down the hallway to the master bedroom.

It was a pleasant room with an adjoining bath. The walls were painted a soft beige and the bedspread was beige with stripes the color of ripe peaches. "You know, if you want to change the colors or styles of any of the rooms, it's definitely something we can discuss," she said.

"So far I find your decorating style quite nice," he replied. "Why don't you use the restroom first to change or whatever, and I'll use it after you're done."

As she went into the bathroom, Jerod sat on the edge of the bed and looked around. There were plenty of framed photos of Caleb at various ages on one wall. A television set was on one side of the dresser, and the other side held bottles of lotions and perfumes and an earring holder.

Both nightstands held dainty lamps, but one additionally held several candles, and the other had a clock radio and a book. He assumed that was the side of the bed she normally slept on, because the lamp was lit and the book held a paper bookmark.

Although he would have preferred to sleep on that side because it was the closest to the doorway in case of an intruder, he wasn't going to force any changes on her. The fact that he was going to be in her bed tonight was change enough.

The bathroom door opened, and she stepped out clad in a knee-length navy blue nightshirt with a gold half-moon on the chest and the words *Sleep Tight* beneath it. Her face was void of makeup, and her hair appeared soft and silky. She looked utterly charming.

"Your turn," she said as she scurried to the bed. She pulled the spread down and slid beneath the peach-colored sheet as if the hot flames of hell were just behind her.

"Be right back," he replied. He carried his duffel bag into the small room, and the first thing he did was brush his teeth, and then he added his toothbrush to the ceramic holder next to hers. He then placed his shaving kit and hairbrush on the back of the toilet and kicked his duffel beneath the freestanding sink to be put away in the morning.

Eventually he needed to get all his clothes and personal items from the Holiday Ranch and move it all in here. But he hadn't wanted to do it before the wedding actually took place.

He changed into a clean white T-shirt and returned to the bedroom. She had the sheet pulled up and tight around her neck, as if she still didn't trust that he just wanted to sleep. He sat on the edge on his side of the bed and pulled off his boots and socks, and then shucked his jeans, leaving him clad in his T-shirt and a pair of black boxers.

He slid beneath the sheets and then turned to look at her. "You okay?" he asked softly.

She offered him a small smile. "I'm fine, just really tired. Getting married is hard work," she said with a small laugh.

Despite her words, he felt the tension radiating from her once again. He knew her tension came from the fact that she didn't trust him yet. And why should she? Despite their legal union, she still didn't really know him. It was going to take time. Eventually he hoped she would come to realize what kind of man he was and he would earn her complete trust.

"I agree that getting married is exhausting," he replied. "So, shall we say good night?"

"Ready for lights out?" she asked.

"Ready."

She reached out and turned off the lamp next to her bed, plunging the room into semidarkness with only the moonlight drifting in through the window. "Good night, Jerod."

"Good night, Lily. I hope you have sweet dreams."

"I hope you do, too," she replied.

What he was really hoping was that they had talked enough and relaxed together enough that she wasn't thinking so much about the doll that had been left hanging on the porch. But he was still thinking about it, and it worried him more than a little bit. What had the person who had left it intended? Was it just a one-shot thing to express some displeasure in them getting married, or was it the beginning of something more insidious and dangerous?

Only time would tell if eventually Lily would learn to trust him. And only time would tell if his new bride was in some kind of danger. With these thoughts in mind, it took him a very long time to finally fall asleep.

Lily awakened to find herself spooned against Jerod's warm body, his arm thrown around her middle. She had to admit to herself that even though it was completely unexpected and a bit shocking, it was also just a little bit more than wonderful. She wasn't in a hurry to move at the moment.

Despite being exhausted the night before, it had taken her a very long time to fall asleep. She'd clung to the edge of the bed and hadn't really relaxed until she heard the deep, even breathing that indicated Jerod had finally gone to sleep.

Her wedding day had been everything she wanted it to be, except for the part where she really didn't know her groom. Still, the ceremony had been so beautiful, and Jerod had been so kind to her. She'd appreciated their talk when they'd gotten home, showing her a glimpse of where he had come from.

It would have been a perfect day if not for that doll. Even now, thinking about it shot a cold shiver up her spine despite the warmth of Jerod's body next to hers.

It had been such a gruesome thing for somebody to leave, and what had been the point? To frighten her? It had certainly succeeded in that. Was it somebody in her life who had left it, or had Jerod lied about his past relationships? Was there a woman in town who was unhappy that he'd gotten married? A woman he was keeping a secret from her?

These new, troubling thoughts finally moved

her out of his arms. Thankfully he didn't awaken. She got up and went into the bathroom where she changed into the same jogging pants and T-shirt she'd had on briefly the night before.

Minutes later she sneaked out of the bedroom and padded down the hallway to the kitchen. She put the coffee on and then walked over to the fridge and opened it. She wondered what her new husband might like for breakfast. Surely he wouldn't turn his nose up at bacon and eggs.

She'd just pulled the bacon out of the refrigerator when he came into the room. "Good morning," he greeted her. "Did you sleep well?"

"I did, what about you?"

"I slept great." He looked so attractive with his hair slightly mussed and clad only in his white T-shirt and a pair of jeans. "I can't believe you made it out of bed without waking me. The smell of the coffee finally woke me."

"I'm glad I didn't disturb you. Help yourself to the coffee. Cups are in the cabinet to the right of the sink. I wasn't sure what you might like for breakfast. I'm making bacon and eggs—is that okay?" she finished, realizing she was in danger of her nerves making her talk too fast and too much.

"That sounds good. I'm not real hard to please when it comes to food." He walked over to the cabinet and pulled down two coffee cups. "Can I pour you a cup?" he asked.

"Oh…yes…thank you."

He set the two cups of coffee on the table. "Now, what can I do to help with breakfast?"

"Nothing. Just sit and enjoy your coffee," she replied. It was strange enough to have him in her kitchen. She didn't want him underfoot as she went about her morning routine. It was going to take a while to get used to the fact that she was now living with a man…a man who was now her husband.

"What time do you expect Caleb to be home today?" he asked.

"Krista said she'd have him home sometime this afternoon. She definitely isn't an early riser on the weekends." She flipped the bacon over and turned to face him. "I told Rod to be available later today to sit down with the two of us to go over everything ranch related."

"I'm looking forward to doing that," he replied. "In fact, I was wondering if maybe after breakfast we could mount up and ride the pastures so you could give me an idea of the property. Do you have a couple of horses?"

"I've got my horse, Daisy, and two others. I love to ride. It's definitely one of my guilty pleasures."

"Me, too. I spoke to Cassie about bringing my

horse from over there to here. I'm going to make arrangements to do that sometime this coming week."

"There's room in the barn for a couple more horses, and in the meantime you're welcome to ride one of mine," she replied and then turned back to the skillet and began to remove the crispy bacon strips.

Minutes later they sat at the table, and while they ate, they small-talked about the weather, the ranch and the ceremony from the day before. She'd always found Jerod rather stern and un-approachable. But she couldn't have been more wrong about him.

He seemed open and easygoing, but she couldn't help but be wary. This man facing her from across the table might be putting on an act and hiding his true nature. Cody had also been open and easygoing until the day he'd emptied her back account, told her how boring she was and completely disappeared from her life.

She knew how crazy the kids at the commu-nity center were about Jerod, and seeing him so open and friendly now let her see the charm she hadn't realized he possessed.

"Do you get to ride a lot?" he asked.

"Not as much as I'd like to. It's hard to get in time when Caleb is here because I don't want to leave him alone in the house, so I usually ride if he's at a friend's house."

"So, this morning is a perfect chance for you to get out and enjoy a ride," he replied with a smile.

When breakfast was over, he helped her with the dishes, and then she went back into the bedroom to change into a pair of jeans for riding. Everything still felt surreal today. It was still hard to believe that she had a husband, a man who planned on living with her and sharing her space for the rest of her life.

It was just after eight when they headed to the barn where the horses were stabled. It was a beautiful day. The sun was bright overhead and the air held a crisp, refreshing chill.

She was surprised to see that beneath Jerod's jacket he wore a holster with a gun. "Expecting trouble?" she asked, her thoughts immediately evoking a mental picture of the mutilated doll.

"Nah, but I never go out on the ranch without a gun to shoot overly aggressive creatures like coyotes or snakes."

They entered the barn. "This is Daisy," she said as they came to the first stall, which held a black mare with a white marking that looked remarkably like a flower. "Then there is Sugar and Brownie."

"They both look like good horseflesh, but Brownie is bigger than Sugar, so I think she'll be my mount for today, if that's okay with you," he said.

"That's fine. I'll warn you, she's a bit spirited."

He flashed her a quick smile. "That's okay, I like my women a little bit spirited."

If that was the case, then he'd definitely married the wrong woman. What spirit she'd once possessed had been stolen away from her by a lying, cheating man. What was left had been beaten out of her by life's disappointments and her own failures. But she wasn't going to think about that anymore. She'd always been a survivor, not a quitter.

Once they were on horseback and he followed her down to the pastures, she felt herself begin to relax. She'd always loved to ride. On the back of a horse was the one place she could almost forget that she'd never had a man who loved her for herself. She could forget that she had a son who was acting out and that she was working a job that wasn't really what she wanted to do with her life.

Jerod looked great in the saddle. With his black cowboy hat on his head, he oozed confidence. His back was straight, his hips rolled easily with the gait of the horse and he held the reins like a pro. They went at a slow pace for a while, and she pointed out various outbuildings, ponds and different elements of the landscape.

"The herd is in the next pasture over," she explained. "We move them back and forth between the two pastures."

"How big is the herd?" he asked.

"Not big enough," she replied. She didn't want to talk about business right now. "Let's really ride," she said to him and then set Daisy off to run.

The brisk breeze blew through her hair as a sweet exhilaration filled her. Laughter bubbled to her lips as she heard Brownie's hooves coming up behind her. She urged Daisy to run faster and threw a glance back at Jerod.

He was laughing as he gained on her. When he reached her side, she slowed Daisy and finally stopped beneath a large maple tree sporting big red autumn leaves. She got off her horse, and he dismounted as well, laughter still riding his lips.

For just a moment as they stood facing each other she felt an unexpected closeness to him even though she knew it was crazy. It had just been a horse ride.

"You're a hell of a rider," he said, admiration in his tone. "You're lucky I didn't have my own horse here or I would have been beneath this tree ten minutes ahead of you."

"Ha! I sense a rematch coming up in the near future, but I have to warn you Daisy was only teasing. She's got a lot more speed in her." Lily sank down in the sweet-smelling grass.

"I'll still ride rings around her with my horse,

Storm," he replied. "How about a little wager?" He sat down next to her.

"What kind of a wager?" she asked.

"If I win, then I win a kiss," he replied.

Her heart fluttered at the thought of him kissing her. She'd only barely tasted his lips ever so briefly at the end of the wedding ceremony the day before. Now she wondered what a real, deep kiss would be like with him. "And what about if I win?" she asked.

He grinned. "Then you win a kiss."

Heat leaped into her cheeks. "Okay, deal," she said.

"You've got some good land here," he said as his gaze went around the area.

"I know," she agreed. "I like to ride to this very spot and sit and relax. I love the smell of the pasture and listening to the sound of the cows."

"Sounds to me like you're a rancher," he replied with another one of his easy smiles.

"Let's remount and I'll show you the herd."

For the next half an hour, they rode among her herd. Thankfully he seemed pleased by what he saw…healthy cattle who grazed peacefully on the last of the summer green grass.

As they headed back to the barn, they talked about winter feed, and she told him about her last-ditch effort to save her ranch by heading to auction next weekend.

"Let's postpone that," he replied when she was finished.

"I'll be glad to as long as my mortgage is paid up and the bank is off my back," she said.

"We're going to take care of that first thing tomorrow morning," he assured her.

There was a part of her that was angry that a man had to rush in to "save" her. The fact that the man was now her husband didn't make it any easier to swallow. She'd always been a strong, independent woman, and this felt so weak and so incredibly desperate. And yet she would do anything to save this ranch for her son.

When they returned to the house, she called Rod to come inside to speak to them. While they waited for the ranch hand, Lily made a fresh pot of coffee and then got the ranch books for the past five years for Jerod to look at.

"You don't have any of this in a computer program?" he asked in surprise.

She set the big financial books in front of him on the table and then set a cup of coffee before him. "No. I've never had the time to transfer the books from paper to computer. I wouldn't even know what kinds of programs I would need to have, and none of the ranch hands I had before Rod knew how to do it. I've just always tried to keep track of things on paper."

"Would you mind if I'd work on getting everything on the computer?"

"Heavens, no." She then poured herself a cup of coffee and joined him at the table. "I should have done it a long time ago, but I just didn't know how to do it all."

"Then I'll start with working on transferring this year's transactions into programs where we can track everything more easily."

"That sounds wonderful," she replied. Nerves shot through her as he opened the records for the past year and began to inspect them.

A frown creased his forehead, a frown that instantly twisted her stomach. "What?" she asked.

He looked up at her. "Relax, Lily."

"You're frowning," she replied.

"It's a frown of concentration." He smiled at her. "What are you worried about?"

"I'm afraid you're going to yell at me for doing everything wrong," she replied.

"Even if I found out a hundred things you've done wrong, I would never yell at you. Lily, I really am a good guy."

She held his gaze for a long moment. "I've put all my trust into believing that's true," she finally replied.

"And I'll prove to you that you haven't made a mistake with me," he replied.

Before either of them could say anything more,

a knock sounded on the back door. "That should be Rod." She got up from the table and greeted the tall, lanky blond who had been working for her for the past three years.

She knew the man was thirty years old, lived in a small apartment in town and had always been very reliable. He'd been invited to the wedding but hadn't shown up. She made the introductions between the two men.

"So, you're the new man in Lily's life," Rod said and held out his hand to Jerod, who had stood when Rod had come in. "It's nice to meet you, Mr. Steen."

"Make it Jerod. We're going to be working together, and I don't stand on formalities."

"Then Jerod it is," Rod replied. The two men shook hands, and then everyone sat down.

For the next hour, Jerod asked questions to both her and Rod about ranch practices, feed and other supplies. Lily explained that Rod did the ordering of the supplies based on what was needed. He'd had a credit card to take care of things, but it had eventually been maxed out, and now she gave him cash for what they needed.

"I've tried to do everything right for Lily," Rod said and smiled at her. "I admire her a lot and have only wanted her to succeed."

"Thanks, Rod," she said, oddly uncomfortable by the warmth of his smile. Had he always looked at her that way, or was she just super-sensitive because of what Caleb had told her about the man?

"So, what do you think?" Lily asked when Rod was gone.

"Did you get receipts from Rod each time he bought something?" Jerod asked.

She frowned. "I tried to, but to be honest, in the past six months or so we got pretty sloppy about it. Why?"

"Either Rod is just ignorant and doesn't know the price of things and the folks at the feed store are taking advantage of him, or he's fleecing you," he said.

She stared at him as her heart plummeted in her chest. "Even if either scenario is true, ultimately it's my fault. I'm the one who has been ignorant about current prices, and if Rod has been cheating me, it's because I've been allowing it. It's also possible I didn't always write down everything he bought on any given day." She released a deep, weary sigh. "Should I let him go?"

"No, I'm willing to give him the benefit of the doubt for right now, at least until I get a better opportunity to go through your records. And to be honest, I'm going to need him to help me with inventory and everything else I need to learn about the ranch."

She released another sigh. "I'm feeling just a bit overwhelmed right now."

Jerod reached across the table and covered her hand with his. His hands were big and strong and callused from hard work. "You are no longer in this by yourself, Lily. We're in this together. We're a team, and I can't wait for us to turn things around so you are finally living your real dream."

She wanted to believe him. She wanted to believe him so badly. But since last night, since the discovery of that horrible, evil-looking doll, she'd had a bad feeling about this whole thing. It was as if the doll was a horrible curse and she was just waiting to see what terrible thing might happen next.

Chapter 5

It had been a little over a week since Lily had been in her classroom. She'd taken the week off after her wedding, and this morning as she walked through the school's front doors, she felt a sense of her life getting back to some sort of normalcy.

It had been an incredibly busy week. Monday morning, true to his word, Jerod had gone with her to the bank and had paid off the overdue mortgage payments. For the next couple of days, Jerod had moved his items into the house. The closet now held both her and his clothing, indicating a married couple shared the space. His horse was now in the barn, and they'd fallen into a comfortable routine.

Despite the fact that they now lived together as a married couple for the past week, there had been no intimacy between them. Not even a single kiss. And over the past week she'd begun to wonder what a real, passionate kiss from her husband would be like.

She'd also begun to ask herself what difference would it make if they actually made love? After all, they were married, and they both wanted a child. She found him not only kind, but also sexy. And part of what she found sexy about him was how patient and gentle he was being with Caleb, despite her son often being sullen and rude.

He assured her after Caleb went to bed each night that it was just going to take time for all three of them to really bond as a family, and he seemed optimistic that eventually that would happen.

Dillon had stopped by on Tuesday morning to tell them he had no information about the bride doll. The local toy store carried them, but Jay Loggins, the owner of the store, couldn't remember the last time he'd sold one. There had also been no fingerprints or any other evidence to further any kind of an investigation. At least nothing more had happened that had frightened her over the past seven days. She was now thinking that the bride doll was just an isolated incident…either a sick joke or an expression of displeasure that wouldn't go any further.

She and Jerod had spent the week getting to know each other better. In the evenings once Caleb went to sleep, their habit had become to sit in the living room and talk about anything and everything.

She now sank down at her desk, wondering how the kids had done with the substitute teacher who had worked the week before.

"Hey." Carol Jenkins whirled into her classroom. "How goes the newlyweds?" She propped her hip on the top of Lily's desk. "I've always imagined making love to Jerod Steen would be totally mind-blowing. Is it? Come on, confess all."

Lily laughed. "I can't believe you're actually confessing to me that you've imagined making love to my husband."

"Hi, ladies." Krista came into the room. "What's going on?"

"I was just grilling Lily about her new sex life with Jerod," Carol said.

"Oh goody, I got here just in time," Krista said. "So, Lily…do tell."

Lily laughed once again. "You both know a real lady doesn't kiss and tell."

"Oooh, that means the sex must be amazing," Krista replied.

"You both should know marriage is about more than the sex," Lily said.

"Not in the first week," Carol said with a laugh.

"You two are too much," Lily replied.

At that moment the school bell rang, indicating the arrival of the students. "We'll continue this conversation at lunch," Krista said.

Carol stood from the edge of Lily's desk. "And we're going to want details."

Lily was still laughing when her two friends disappeared out of her room. Still, the conversation had stirred a yearning inside her. In sleep, she and Jerod always found each other. She awakened each morning in his arms, even though they never spoke about their sleeping intimacy.

Now she found herself wanting much more intimacy with him. She knew he was just waiting for a signal from her, and maybe tonight she would give him that signal. Suddenly she couldn't wait for nighttime to come.

At lunch Carol and Krista continued to tease her about Jerod until Brad walked into the teachers' lounge. "Well, well…how's the newlywed?" he asked. He sat across from her at the round table and pulled a sandwich out of a brown bag.

"I'm doing fine," she replied.

"You know, Lily, I really wish you would have told me you were open to dating. I could have swept you right off your feet if you'd given me half a chance."

Lily wasn't sure quite how to respond. "What can I say, Brad? Jerod just stole my heart away," she finally said.

"Get off her back, Brad," Krista exclaimed. "Don't be such a jerk."

"I wasn't trying to be a jerk," Brad protested. He gazed at Lily for a long moment. "Seriously, Lily, I'm really glad if you're happy."

Lily smiled at him. "I am happy, Brad...and I hope you and I can continue to be friends and coworkers." For the first time she saw what she believed was a real, genuine smile from the man.

"Okay, let's stop with all the sappy stuff, otherwise I won't be able to keep down my lunch," Krista said, making them all laugh.

The rest of the day went smoothly, and after school Lily waited for Krista to join her as they walked to their cars. Krista's son, Henry, was with her, but once again Caleb had gone home with his friend for more work on their science fair project.

"One more week and the greatest science fair in the entire world will finally happen," Krista said with a bit of sarcasm as she fell into step next to Lily. Henry lagged a bit behind them, already with his cell phone in his hand. Lily's and Krista's vehicles were parked side by side in the teachers' lot.

Lily laughed. "I do think it's going to be a great

event for the school. I've heard they're bringing in judges from one of the schools in Oklahoma City."

"Well, that's good. Maybe little Mikey Brady won't win first place for a change," Krista replied. Terra Brady, mother of fourth-grader Mike Brady, was head of the PTA, and no matter what contest was run at the school, somehow little Mikey always won a prize. "Terra is already probably trying to find out who the judges are so she can bribe them with some of her award-winning pies or cold cash…whatever it takes to keep little Mikey in blue ribbons."

"Be careful, your inner witch is showing," Lily replied with a grin at her friend.

Krista returned her grin. "Takes one to know one."

By that time the two had reached Krista's car and Lily's truck. "Hey, Carol and I are going out Saturday night for a few drinks. Want to come along?"

"Not this time," Lily replied. "I'm not sure Jerod would want me to go out without him."

"Oh, I'm feeling very jealous right now," Krista said. "I wish I had somebody at home who didn't want me to go out without him."

"You'll find that special someone, Krista."

"Mom, can we go?" Henry asked impatiently.

"Yeah, son. We're going now. Lily, I'll see you tomorrow," Krista said.

As Krista and her son got into their car, Lily got into her truck and headed home. Home to Jerod. Strange that her heart already warmed with thoughts of him.

Part of their routine they had set up for when she returned to work was that when she got home, he would probably be out in the pasture or in the barn. He'd been working on inventorying all the supplies she had on hand.

Around five o'clock, he would come inside, and by that time she would have dinner ready and the three of them would sit down to eat. After dinner, Caleb went back to his room, she would work on anything she might have brought home from school and Jerod worked on his computer transferring information from the books to the programs he'd decided to use for ranch business. And then by around ten o'clock, they went to bed and usually went right to sleep.

Tonight she was ready for something different. Her fingers tightened around her steering wheel. So far she had seen no red flags with Jerod. With their evenings together and by sleeping together each night, they had already deepened their intimacy. However, tonight she wanted to take that intimacy even deeper.

She was ready to make love with her husband.

A sweet shiver ran up her spine at the thought of Jerod kissing her deeply, of feeling his big hands on her body. A week ago she hadn't been able to imagine making love with him so soon.

But they had a real marriage, and he was now her real husband, and maybe it was time for them to have a sexual relationship as well as the trust and friendship they had slowly been building since their wedding. Despite the shortness of time, she was ready.

When she reached the turn for the ranch, she stopped at the mailbox. She was surprised that along with the usual bills and junk mail, there was a brown mailing envelope that held something soft. It had no address, indicating that somebody had just put it in the mailbox without actually mailing it.

Maybe it was a late wedding present. Even though she and Jerod had specifically indicated no gifts when they invited everyone to the wedding, they had still received a few.

Krista had bought them a beautiful silver serving platter, and the teachers from the school had gotten them a set of dishes. The cowboys at the Holiday Ranch had gone together and bought them a fancy coffee maker that not only made coffee, but also made iced tea and other drinks.

She now drove on to the house and parked her truck and then headed into the house. She carried the mail to the kitchen, which smelled of chicken and vegetables. Thank goodness she'd put everything into a slow cooker that morning so dinner was basically ready. All she intended to do was bake some biscuits to go with the meal.

She sat at the table with the package in front of her. It felt soft, and she couldn't imagine what might be inside. She tore at the brown mailing bag, and when she got it open she pulled out a pair of men's navy boxers. *What the heck?* She stared at the boxers for a long moment, trying to make sense of why somebody would put them in her mailbox.

She checked the bag and realized there was a note inside. She pulled it out, and as she read it her heart began to thunder.

Thank you, my sweet prince, for this afternoon. I thought you might need these back. There's nothing better than a little afternoon delight.

She read the words over and over again, as if somehow, if she read them enough times, they might change. Today was the first day since they'd married that she'd gone to work, leaving Jerod on his own for the day. And this was what he'd done with his afternoon?

As she folded the note, grief crashed through her. She'd spent the day anticipating making love to him, but apparently he had already had sex with somebody else. Along with the grief was a deep sense of betrayal.

She shoved the items back into the bag and then carried it into her bedroom and put it in the very back of her underwear drawer. She wasn't ready to give it to Jerod and confront him. She sank down on the edge of her bed and tears pressed hot at her eyes.

How dare he? She had trusted him. How could he do this to her? Why had he married her if he had a relationship...was having sex with another woman? Who else knew that he had another woman, that he was now having an affair? God, she was probably the laughingstock of the whole town. She swallowed hard against all the emotions that threatened to erupt.

She intended to confront him about this, just not now. Caleb would be home soon, and she needed to get her emotions completely under control before she told Jerod to pack his stuff and get out of her house.

Jerod knew something was wrong after being in the house for a few minutes. Lily was unusually quiet, and the sparkle he'd come to anticipate in her eyes was gone.

"How was work today?" he asked her when they all sat down to eat.

"It was fine," she replied rather sharply. She didn't even look at him.

"What about you, Caleb? Did you have a good day?" Jerod turned his attention to Caleb. Hopefully, eventually Lily would talk to him about whatever seemed to be bothering her. But he wasn't going to press her, especially in front of Caleb.

"I had a good day," Caleb replied. "You should see what my science project is, Jerod. It's going to be so cool."

"You want to tell me what it is or do you want me to just see it at the science fair?" Jerod asked.

"Are you going to come to the science fair?" Caleb asked him in obvious surprise.

"Of course I am. Caleb, I know you don't want me to be your dad, but I consider you my son and I want to go to all your school functions," Jerod said.

Caleb looked at him for a long moment and then he slowly nodded. "Cool," he replied.

Jerod looked at Lily and was surprised to see a flash of anger in her eyes. She glared at him then quickly looked down at her plate. What was going on with her? Something must have happened at school today. He couldn't imagine what she'd be angry with him about, but he wouldn't know what it was unless she shared with him.

She continued to be cool and distant through

the rest of the meal. He small-talked with Caleb as they all cleared the dishes. "Why don't we do something different tonight and spend a little family time together," he suggested before Caleb could disappear to his room.

It bothered him each night when the boy would isolate himself in his room to play video games and there was no real together time with the three of them. They couldn't really bond together as a family if they never spent any quality time together.

"What do you want to do?" Caleb asked curiously.

"Do you have any games we could play in the living room?" Jerod asked.

"I'm sorry, but I have a headache and don't feel like doing anything other than going to lie down," Lily said.

"Is there anything I can do?" Jerod asked in concern. Was that what was wrong with her? A headache?

"No, I just need some quiet time." She walked out of the kitchen and disappeared down the hallway.

"Does your mother get headaches a lot?" Jerod asked Caleb once she was gone.

"I don't think so, but I'm usually in my room for most of the time after school. So…do you still want to do something?" Caleb asked tentatively.

"Sure. Do you know any card games?"

Caleb grinned. "I know how to play poker."

"Whoa, where did you learn that?"

"Krista taught me and Henry, and sometimes when I'm spending time with them, we all play poker together," Caleb replied. "Krista told me I'm good at it."

Jerod grinned at the boy. "We'll see how good you are. Let me grab some matchsticks and a deck of cards and let's go play some poker," Jerod said. Even though he wasn't sure that playing poker was the best thing to do with a young boy, he was just glad that Caleb was willing to engage with him at all.

He opened the cabinet where he'd seen a deck of cards and a package of long matchsticks he assumed Lily used to start the barbecue grill on the back porch.

Together he and Caleb went into the living room. Jerod sat on the sofa, and Caleb sank down on the floor on the other side of the coffee table. Jerod moved the artificial flower arrangement from the center of the coffee table, and then he dealt the first hand.

As they played the first couple of hands, Caleb crowed with success as his cards turned out better than Jerod's and he gathered his winning matchsticks into a pile.

Jerod found himself torn between the fun with

Caleb and his concern for Lily. But at the moment there was nothing he could do for Lily, and so he gave himself to spending this time with Caleb.

For the first time since the wedding, Caleb was really talking to him as they played. He mentioned how much he wanted to fish the pond on the property and that he wanted a horse of his own so he could learn how to ride. He also confessed that he was a little bit scared of the dark and that he loved to dip potato chips into chocolate ice cream.

Jerod listened more than he talked, and when eight o'clock rolled around, he told Caleb they'd play one more game and then it was probably time for Caleb to get in the shower.

"You know, I could see about us getting you a horse and I could teach you how to ride, or I'd be glad to take you fishing if you want me to," Jerod said.

Caleb stared at him for a long moment, his blue eyes losing the laughter and instead becoming dark and troubled. It was as if he flipped a switch in his head. He tossed down his cards and got up. "I'll go take my shower now."

As he raced from the room, Jerod tried to figure out what he'd said wrong, but he couldn't think of anything. All he'd done was offer to do things with Caleb that he had indicated he wanted to do.

There must be something in the air, Jerod thought as he put the matchsticks and the cards away. First Lily and now Caleb. He walked down the hallway and was just about to reach the bedroom door when Lily opened it. "Lily, are you feeling better?"

"Not really." She stepped past him. "I just came out to tuck Caleb into bed."

"Is there anything I can do to make you feel better?" For the first time he realized her eyes were slightly swollen and red-rimmed. Was her headache pain so bad it had her crying? "Do you get these headaches often?"

"No, only under certain circumstances," she replied. Once again her tone was curt as she headed down the hallway and directly to Caleb's room.

Jerod went back to the living room to lock the front door and turn out all the lights. He didn't know how to help his wife, and he didn't know how to help Caleb. The one thing he did know was that first thing in the morning, he intended to drive into town and get a night-light for Caleb's room.

No child who was afraid of the dark should have to be in his room at night without a little light to soothe his fear. Maybe Caleb had never told his mother about his fear, but Jerod knew now and intended to do something about it.

He went into the bedroom to get ready for bed. Each night when he got into bed with Lily, he was tantalized by the soft lilac scent that emanated from her. He found himself wondering more and more what it would be like to kiss her fully and deeply. He fantasized about how her naked body would feel against his own.

But he'd vowed to be patient where the physical side of their relationship was concerned. Over the past week he'd believed they had been working on deepening their trust, their friendship with each other. And hopefully, eventually, that would open up their physical relationship.

He sank down on the edge of the bed to await Lily's return to the room. He wanted to share with her what Caleb had told him, but more importantly, he wanted to know if there was anything he could do for her.

She came into the bedroom, and he patted the bed next to him. "Lily, can you sit down and talk to me for a minute?"

"No, I can't. I'm going to change into my nightgown, and then I'm going to sleep," she replied. Her tone was once again sharp, and she made no eye contact with him before she went into the bathroom and slammed the door behind her.

Jerod frowned. He had the distinct feeling that Lily was angry with him, but he didn't know why. All he could do was try to talk to her when she got out of the bathroom. If she was angry with him for some reason, he needed to know why so he could fix it.

When she came back in the room, once again she didn't look at him. She got into bed and faced away from him. "Is your headache any better?" he asked softly.

"It's fine."

"Lily, if your pain is really bad, maybe you should call your doctor."

"I said it was fine."

He hesitated a moment, staring at her back. "Caleb and I played cards this evening, and I really enjoyed spending time with him," he said. "He's such a bright kid."

She didn't reply.

"Lily, it's obvious that something is wrong and you're upset with me. Do you want to tell me what's going on?"

She turned over and sat up, and when her gaze met his, her eyes burned with an anger that was palpable. "I'll tell you what is going on." Tears began to fill her eyes. "I want a divorce."

Chapter 6

Jerod looked at her in stunned surprise. "A...a divorce?" He stuttered over the words.

She nodded, new tears blurring her vision as her heart squeezed so tight in her chest she could scarcely breathe. She had spent all evening playing and replaying the note and the boxers in her head.

She'd been such a fool to trust any man again. She'd come into this marriage with good intentions to make it work, but he apparently hadn't had those same good intentions. He was just another liar and cheater like Cody had been. The only difference was Cody hadn't married her.

"Lily, what are you saying? What's happened that you want to divorce me?" He stared at her as if she'd lost her mind.

"You should know." She swiped angrily at the tears. "What did you do this afternoon while I was at work?"

He was such a good actor, she thought, as he appeared completely bewildered. "I worked in the barn to get things more organized."

"And then maybe you sneaked away for a little afternoon delight?" How could he be so brazen not to just admit what was going on?

"Afternoon delight?" He continued to stare at her. "Lily, what in the hell are you talking about?"

She threw the sheet off her and got out of the bed. "I'll not only tell you what I'm talking about…I'll show you." She walked over to her dresser and pulled out the brown mailing envelope. She threw it at his head. "That's what I'm talking about."

He ducked and the package sailed over his head. He picked it up with one eye on her, as if unsure what else to expect from her. He pulled the boxers out, a frown cutting deep across his forehead. "What is this?"

"It was in the mailbox today. Don't play stupid with me, Jerod," she replied angrily. "Oh, and don't forget to read the lovely note that came with the boxers."

He pulled out the note and read it and then threw it onto the bed. "This is a bunch of bull. Lily, somebody is trying to make trouble between us. I wasn't with any woman this afternoon. You can ask Rod. Call and ask him. He was with me all afternoon. I wouldn't do something like that. I would never do anything like that." His deep, ragged voice sounded like the truth.

She stared at him. For the first time, a small edge of doubt crept into her head. Was it possible he really was telling the truth? Was it possible the same person who had left the mutilated bride doll had done this to create an issue between them?

"Lily, I'm an honorable man, and I would never, ever cheat on you. I take my vows very seriously. You're my wife, and I would never do something like this to dishonor you." He stood and took her by the hand. She allowed him to lead her back to the bed, where they both sat down.

"Lily, I swear to you, those aren't my boxers, and there is no woman. You should have come to me the minute you saw what was in this package," he said softly.

She buried her face in her hands as tears nearly overwhelmed her. "I... I was t-too mortified," she finally managed to choke out. Now she was mortified because she knew she should have immediately spoken to him, maybe should have given him the benefit of the doubt.

However, she believed him now. Rod would never be a willing accomplice to Jerod's lies. If Jerod said he'd been working all afternoon with Rod, then it was easy enough for her to check.

"You should have trusted in me, Lily." He took her hands and gently pulled them down from her face. He used his thumbs to swipe away her tears, his dark eyes looking tortured.

She looked down at her lap, unable to meet his gaze with so many emotions rushing through her. "Yes, I probably should have, but there hasn't been enough time to build that kind of trust between us."

"What I'd like to know is who would do such a malicious thing? Who would go to such great lengths to manufacture such a lie about me to make you believe I betrayed you like this?" There was an edge of anger in his voice, an anger she now identified with.

"You said you were dating Donna Maddox for a little while. I don't know her very well—is she the kind of woman who would do something like this?" she asked.

"I can't imagine her doing something like this...and for what? I haven't dated her in months and months. She would know that breaking us up isn't going to make me date her again. What about Brad?"

A deep sigh escaped her. "I thought Brad and I

had turned a corner today." She told him about her conversation with him at lunch that day. "Maybe he was being nice because he knew this was going to ruin things for me."

"Surely he knows that if he destroys our marriage you still wouldn't be interested in getting together with him," Jerod replied.

"I don't know what he thinks. I just can't wrap my head around somebody who would do something like this. It's just so...so wicked."

"It's obvious somebody out there doesn't want us to be together. Whoever it is, they're playing dirty. What we need to do is stand united. I want you to come to me if anything like this happens again, and I'll come to you immediately if somebody tries to malign your character. Deal?"

"Deal," she replied.

"Do you want me to call Dillon?"

"No." The idea of anyone else knowing about this totally appalled her. "I'm sure the person who put that in the mailbox didn't leave any fingerprints or anything else that might help identify them. There's really nothing Dillon can do, and I would prefer that nobody know about this."

His dark gaze held hers intently. "Lily, I will never, ever cheat on you. I will never steal from you or do anything to dishonor you. I swear to you, I'm just not that kind of man."

In the very depths of her heart, she believed

him. She should have shown him what was in the package the minute she received it. But trust had only just begun to build with her, and it had been far easier to doubt him.

"I'm sorry, Jerod. I'm sorry I doubted you," she said. "I just saw what was in the package, and I felt so betrayed...so angry that I couldn't even think straight."

"It's okay, I just don't want you to ever doubt me again in the future. I'm on your side always." He reached up and swiped an errant strand of hair off the side of her face.

His touch was so tender, and as he leaned closer to her, her heart suddenly hitched in her chest. And then his lips were on hers in a sweet kiss that quickened her heartbeat and made all the tension in her body melt away.

Just when she thought he'd pull back and end the kiss, she reached up and wrapped her arms around his neck. Immediately his tongue tentatively sought entry, and she allowed it, opening her mouth to him.

Suddenly the kiss wasn't just about a simple connection. It was about desire. He kissed her like he meant it, like he wanted it, and the taste of that desire on his lips thrilled her.

The kiss continued for several wonderful minutes, and then he finally drew back from her and she dropped her arms from around his neck. "Why don't we call it a night," he said.

She nodded, her emotions all over the place. On the one hand, she was disappointed that the kiss hadn't been followed up by more intimacy, but on the other hand, she understood him not wanting to go there, considering how she'd come at him earlier. Besides, when they did eventually make love, she wanted it to be without her emotional baggage weighing her down.

She was completely exhausted from her anger, her heartache and all the tears she had shed. By the time they both got into the bed, she was ready to go to sleep.

She closed her eyes and tried not to think about the fact that somebody in or around town wanted to destroy the happiness she and Jerod were trying to build together.

Who had been behind the doll? And who had left the boxers and the note in the mailbox? And more importantly, what might happen next?

The rest of the week passed without anything else happening to ruin their growing relationship. Once again there had been no more intimacy between them, but Lily felt herself growing closer to Jerod with each day that passed.

They had begun to spend their evenings together as a family, and Caleb was spending far less time isolated in his room. It felt good to play games and laugh together like a real family. Twice in the evenings, Jerod had taken Caleb to the community center, and when they got home, the three of them sat at the table and ate ice cream.

Caleb was definitely warming up to Jerod, and that touched her heart. Jerod had not only bought her son a night-light for his room, but this morning they were surprising Caleb with a horse of his own. The horse was already in one of the stalls in the barn.

The day began as most Saturdays did for her. She fried bacon and made pancakes for all of them. "Are you really coming to the science fair on Thursday night?" Caleb asked Jerod once they were seated at the table.

"I'm really coming," Jerod replied. "I can't wait to see your project. Do you want to give me any hints about it?"

Caleb frowned thoughtfully. "It's earth-shattering," he replied and then giggled.

Lily hugged the sound of her son's giggles deep inside her heart. She gave Jerod the credit for bringing her son's laughter back to her. Caleb hadn't had a single temper fit in the past week. He hadn't once complained about missing his evening video-game time.

"Hmm, earth-shattering," Jerod mused. "Are you setting off dynamite?"

"No," Caleb said with another laugh. "That would be dangerous."

"Totally," Jerod replied. "So, have you invented a new flavor of tortilla chip? That would be earth-shattering for some people."

"You're being goofy," Caleb said to Jerod.

Jerod grinned. "Yes, I am. I can sometimes be a goofy guy. Now we need to finish up breakfast, because your mother and I have a big surprise for you."

"What kind of a surprise?" Caleb sat up straighter in his chair and looked at Lily and then back at Jerod.

"It's earth-shattering," Jerod said, and Lily laughed along with her son.

"Then let's all eat fast so I can see my surprise," Caleb said.

When they'd finished eating and had cleared up the dishes, they all three walked out of the house. "Wait here," Jerod said to Caleb before they got to the barn.

"What is it, Mom?" Caleb asked as he stared after Jerod.

"Just wait and see," Lily replied. She should have done this a long time ago. She would have already taught Caleb how to ride, but none of the horses she owned were appropriate for a new, young rider, and she hadn't had the extra money to go out and buy one.

Thankfully Jerod had found the horse he thought perfect, and he'd paid for it. She couldn't wait to see Caleb's reaction now. She just knew he was going to be absolutely thrilled.

Jerod appeared minutes later, leading out the new mare for Caleb. The horse was smaller boned than any of Lily's horses, and according to Abe Breckenridge, who had sold her to them, the mare was sweet-tempered and docile.

"This is now officially your horse, son," Jerod said. "Her name is Diamond, and your saddle even has your name on it. See right here? I figured we could start right away to teach you how to ride. What do you think?"

Lily waited for her son to jump up and down, to clap his hands together in excitement. Instead, he stared at Jerod for a long moment. His eyes darkened. "I don't want the dumb horse," he yelled, and then he raced into the barn.

Lily's heart squeezed tight. What had just happened? What was wrong with Caleb? How could they really become a family when she didn't know what was going on with her son?

Jerod was aware of Lily following behind him as he went into the barn to find Caleb. Of all the reactions he'd expected from Caleb, the one he had gotten had shocked him.

It had only been a little over a week ago that

Caleb had told him he wanted a horse of his own and that he wanted to learn how to ride. Why had Caleb rejected the horse now? What was going on in the little boy's head?

"Caleb?" Jerod walked into the barn and looked around, but he saw no sign of the boy anywhere. He was apparently hiding. "Caleb, where are you? We need to talk."

"I don't want to talk." Caleb's voice came from an empty horse stall on the left. "Just leave me alone."

"I can't do that, Caleb."

"Why not?"

Jerod exchanged a look with Lily and then moved closer to the stall. "I need to talk to you because I care about you."

"Why should you care about me? My own father didn't care enough about me to even get to know me. He didn't want me, so why should you?" A stark pain and rage radiated from Caleb's voice. "And you probably won't stick around, either. I'm just not lovable. I'm no good."

"Oh, Caleb…" Lily started to rush forward, but Jerod stopped her with a hand on her arm. Right now Caleb didn't need his mother. He knew his mother loved him.

Jerod knew intimately the kind of anger and pain Caleb was feeling, and Jerod believed this was the source of Caleb's temper fits. Jerod was the best person to talk to the boy right now.

"Hey, buddy, it sucks about your dad," Jerod said. "My father left me when I was a year old. So, he even got to meet me and still took off." Jerod took a couple of steps closer to the stall. "And then when I was fifteen, my mom tried to kill me." Lily's gasp was audible behind him, but he stayed focused on the hurting little boy in the horse stall.

"She tried to kill you?" Caleb's voice had lost some of the rage. "Why did she do that?"

"Can I come in and sit down with you?" Jerod asked.

There was a long moment of silence. "Okay," Caleb finally agreed.

Jerod stepped into the stall, where Caleb was curled up in the corner. Jerod sank down in the hay facing Caleb. "After my dad took off, my mother started drinking and taking drugs. Do you know about drugs?"

"Yeah, I know they're really bad."

"They are, and so is drinking too much alcohol."

Caleb's blue eyes stared at Jerod. "And your mom did those things?"

"She did." Jerod hoped he wasn't going wrong in sharing with Caleb something he'd never shared with anyone else. It was something that was ugly and exposed the rawness of what life sometimes had to offer.

"So, why did she try to kill you?"

"I don't think she ever liked me much. She didn't take good care of me, and then when I was fifteen, she was dating a very bad man. One night they were both drunk and on drugs and fighting, and he started to beat up my mom. When I tried to stop him, my mother broke her beer bottle and used it to cut down the side of my face. Then she told me if I didn't leave she was going to kill me, so I left."

Jerod reached up and touched the scar that had been left behind. He took several deep, long breaths as a rush of unexpected emotions blew through him. His chest tightened and his mouth dried as he remembered that horrible time.

That night his mother had become a monster. He'd never forget the hatred that had shone from her eyes as she had sliced down his face and then threatened to stab him in the heart if he didn't leave her boyfriend alone. She had chosen a man who beat her over her son. She'd always chosen drugs and men over him.

He only realized he had gotten caught up in the old memories when Caleb's small hand covered his and pulled him back to the here and now. "I guess sometimes we just get bad parents," Caleb said. "But you're lucky. You have a mom who loves you with all her heart, and you have me, Caleb. I'll always be here, loving and supporting you as long as your mom and you want me to." He turned his hand over and squeezed Caleb's. "Now, what do you say we both get out of this barn stall and I really introduce you to your new horse?"

"Okay," Caleb replied. The two of them both stood, but before they left the stall, Jerod stopped him.

"Caleb, any time you want to talk about your disappointment and your anger about your dad, come to me. I'll always listen to you because I really understand. Deal?"

Once again Caleb looked up at Jerod for a long moment, and then he nodded. "Deal."

As they came out of the stall, Jerod didn't quite meet Lily's eyes. He knew she'd heard everything he'd said, and the last thing he wanted to see in his wife's eyes was pity.

They went back outside where, thankfully, Diamond still stood in the same place. Jerod took the reins and led the horse into the corral. "Before we can get you riding, you need to make friends with Diamond."

Caleb eyed him curiously. "Make friends how?"

"Let her smell you and stroke down her nose. Rub down her neck and let her get used to you."

As Caleb began to interact with Diamond, Jerod moved to stand next to Lily. She surprised him by taking his hand in hers, and when he looked at her, there was no pity in her eyes. Instead there was a warmth that half stole his breath away. She held his hand for only a moment and then released it, and he immediately missed her touch.

For the next couple of hours, Jerod worked with Caleb and Diamond. Lily leaned on the corral railing and watched them. It was like a dream Jerod had envisioned for himself for years…his wife watching him while he taught his son to ride. It didn't matter that Caleb was a stepson. He was Jerod's family now, and that's all that mattered.

It was strange to him that before the marriage he hadn't paid much attention to Lily Kidwell, but since the marriage he'd noticed a lot of things about her. Like the fact that her hair wasn't just a plain brown, but in the sunlight it sparkled with interesting strands of red and gold. He knew how sweet her lips tasted, but he'd never noticed before how lush they looked.

The more time he spent with her, the more he noticed how pretty she was, and the more he desired her.

He loved the sound of her laughter, which was melodious and infectious. He liked that she was a cheerful morning person and the way she loved her son. He could easily imagine her as the mother of his children, but there was a little part of him that believed this was all too good to be true.

For the first fifteen years of his life, he had been told he wasn't important, that he didn't matter and therefore he didn't deserve any real happiness. He'd seen himself as a worthless, unlovable kid.

Despite the years with Big Cass, there were still times when those early childhood memories haunted him and inner demons rose up that told him he'd never be good enough, he'd never be smart enough to please anyone.

He shook his head to now dispel those demons and instead focused on Caleb and Lily. Thank God, he and Lily had gotten through the boxer issue, although he'd still like to know who had tried to tear him and his new wife apart.

He and Caleb worked with the horse until noon, when they all went inside for lunch. Over sandwiches Caleb chattered excitedly about getting in the saddle that afternoon. There was no hint of the sad, angry child they had seen earlier in the day.

In the afternoon Jerod put Caleb in the saddle and worked teaching him how to guide a horse with a nudge of his knees and a slight tug on the reins. They stayed in the corral, and right before dinner the three of them saddled up and went for a slow ride through the pasture.

Caleb did great, but as always Jerod's eyes kept drifting to Lily. Clad in a light blue sweater and jeans, and with a wide smile on her face, she looked absolutely beautiful.

There had been no more intimacy between them since the kiss they'd shared after the boxer incident. That kiss had been amazing and he was eager to do it again, but he was still afraid to make a move on his own. He needed her to take the lead where their intimacy was concerned. With each day that passed, he was more and more drawn to her.

By the time supper came and went, Caleb was exhausted from the day in the fresh air and his excitement over Diamond. They decided not to play games that evening. Caleb just wanted to shower and get ready for bed.

"Wow, this is unusual, especially on a Saturday night," Lily said at seven thirty, when Caleb had been tucked in and was sound asleep.

Jerod sank down on the sofa next to her. "It was a good day. He was a fast study on the horse."

"Now we'll have trouble keeping him off Diamond," she replied. Her eyes sparkled with her happiness, and desire for her punched Jerod in the pit of his stomach. There was no better feeling in the world than seeing your wife happy, he thought.

"We need to set up some rules, and right now the main one should be that he doesn't ride alone. He's nowhere near ready for that."

Lily smiled at him. "I agree."

He returned her smile. "It's nice to be on the same page when it comes to rules."

"Totally nice." She moved a little closer to him, bringing with her that soft lilac scent that he found so evocative. "Thank you for sharing with him this morning. I had no idea that Caleb had such terrible feelings about his father...about himself."

"I think it's the source of the anger issues he's been having. Hopefully talking about it will ease some of that anger," Jerod replied.

Lily placed a hand on his thigh. "Yes, but I think you sharing what happened to you as a kid really helped him, and for that I thank you. It couldn't have been easy for you to talk about those things."

"It was a very dark time," he admitted.

"Was your mother always abusive with you?" she asked. Her eyes were soft pools of comfort. He wanted to dive in and live in them.

"Yeah, she'd beaten and neglected me throughout my childhood, but that night it was something different. I'd never really gotten in between her and one of her loser boyfriends before, but that night I thought he was going to kill her, and so I hit her boyfriend in the jaw to get him off her."

He ran his hand down his scar and then dropped his hand back to his lap. "And I not only got this for my trouble, but I really believed she wanted to kill me that night. I knew then I had to leave. If her boyfriend didn't wind up killing her, then the drugs she was doing were going to, and I couldn't stick around to watch it even if she wanted me to, which she didn't. She made it clear that night how much she resented me…how much she hated me."

"Oh, Jerod, I'm so very sorry for you. Have you seen or heard from her since that night?"

"No. Even if I wanted to find her, I would have no clue where to look. If she wasn't running away from the law, she was running away from bill collectors. We never stayed in one place for long. I don't know if she's still in the state of Oklahoma or if she's dead." He released a deep sigh. "And now let's talk about something more pleasant."

They spent the rest of the evening watching a sitcom and talking about their visions for the ranch. He continued to be acutely aware of the enticement of her warmth and her scent so close to him.

When he'd made the proposition to Lily about marrying him, he'd never dreamed there would come a time when he would desire her as much as he did now. He'd never dreamed he would want to make love to her aside from impregnating her so he could have a child of his own.

However, at the moment, he wasn't thinking about getting her pregnant—he was thinking about how much he'd like to take her mouth with his, how much he wanted to undress her and kiss each and every inch of skin he exposed.

He tamped down the arousal his thoughts were evoking. No matter how much desire he felt for her, he didn't intend to act on it. She was going to have to show him when she was ready for it to happen.

Still, he felt a new kind of intimacy with her given what he'd shared about his mother. She now knew his dirty, ugly past, and if she decided to reject him because of it, then it would be nothing more than what he expected.

Rather than reject him, she had made him feel closer to her, and he was certain he had picked a woman far different from the one who had given birth to him.

Lily would never turn on her son. She would never, ever allow a man to come between herself and her son, and those were the values he had wanted in his woman…in the woman who would be the mother to his children if this marriage worked out.

At nine o'clock she turned off the television, and he shut off the lights and made sure the doors were locked up tight. She checked on Caleb, who was still sleeping soundly, and then together they went down the hallway to their bedroom.

Lily changed into her nightgown first, and then Jerod went into the bathroom to brush his teeth and get undressed for bed. He was surprised when he came back into the bedroom to find Lily propped up on her pillow, as if she wasn't ready to go directly to sleep.

"On the whole, this was the best day ever," she said as he slid into the bed next to her.

He smiled at her. "On a scale from one to ten, this was definitely a nine."

She raised an eyebrow. "Only a nine?"

He nodded. "A ten is for something unbelievingly wonderful. So far, I've never had a ten."

She scooted a little closer to him and reached out and ran her fingers down his scar. He froze in stunned surprise. Her fingers were so soft, so tender against the shame of his past.

"I hate that this happened to you," she murmured. "And yet if it hadn't happened, you wouldn't be here now with me." She dropped her hand but didn't move away from him.

He'd worried about seeing pity in her gaze, but instead he saw something else—a burn…a raw desire that accelerated his heartbeat. Her mouth was slightly open, as if in invitation.

He leaned forward and captured her mouth with his, and all he tasted was sweet desire and open acceptance. He wanted this woman—his wife—with a passion that stole his breath away.

When the kiss ended, she leaned back from him, her eyes blazing with a fire that made his heart race even faster. He wanted to pull her against him. He wanted to strip the nightgown off her body and love her nakedness. But he did none of those things. The last thing he wanted to do was move too fast for her. Instead, he froze and waited to see what would happen next.

She held his gaze for another long moment. "I want you, Jerod. I want you to make love to me." She leaned over and turned off the lamp, and then she was back in his arms.

Chapter 7

Lily's desire for her husband had been building over the last couple of days, but today when he'd opened up and become so vulnerable to help her son with his emotions, it had shot her desire for Jerod over the moon.

It had been such a joy to watch him work with Caleb and the horse in the corral. He'd been so patient and he'd looked so incredibly hot with his black hat set at a handsome angle on his head and the worn jeans that fit so well on his long legs and across his incredible butt.

She'd never felt special or sexy, but as she saw the heated glow in Jerod's eyes in the moonlight that drifted through the window, she felt both sexy and very desirable.

She moved back into his arms, and their mouths found each other in a kiss that stole her breath and raced shivers of pleasure up her spine. Her husband definitely knew how to kiss. His tongue swirled with hers, and her heartbeat raced in anticipation of what would come next.

They kissed for several long moments, and then she began to tug on the bottom of his T-shirt. She wanted to slide her hands across the wide expanse of the muscled flesh of his chest.

He reared back from her and pulled the T-shirt over his head and tossed it to the floor on the side of the bed. In the moonlight his chest was bronzed and beautiful. He had a small smattering of dark hair that narrowed and disappeared into the top of his boxers.

Immediately she ran her hands over the warm expanse of skin as his lips slid down her cheek and then glided down to kiss her throat. The warmth of his mouth felt incredibly good.

She was on fire with her want…with her need for her husband. It had been so long since she'd made love, so long since she'd felt this kind of passion, of desire. She'd almost forgotten that she was not only a mother and a respected teacher, but she was also a woman. Jerod had awakened something inside her that had been dormant for a very long time.

She not only wanted to caress his warm flesh, but she wanted his touch on her. She wanted to feel the slow slide of his work-roughened hands all over her body. She leaned back from him and, taking a deep breath, she pulled her nightgown over her head and tossed it aside, leaving her clad only in a pair of wispy, silky underpants.

"Lily, you are so beautiful," he murmured. She felt more beautiful than she'd ever felt in her life as he drew her back into his arms. He kissed her, and at the same time his hand stroked across her collarbone and then to her breasts.

His hands were so warm, and her nipples hardened eagerly beneath his touch. She gasped in delight as his mouth moved to lick and kiss first one nipple and then the other. Electric currents coupled with a sweet heat traveled from her breasts to the very center of her.

As his mouth teased and kissed her breasts, his hands skimmed down her stomach and to her upper thighs, further tormenting her with a need that had her half-mad. The want for him crashed into her with a quickness that surprised her. She clutched his shoulders and then reached up to tangle her fingers in his soft hair.

"Lily, are you sure about this?" His voice was

deep and raspy against her ear. "I don't want to rush you. I want you to be very sure."

She looked up into his eyes and smiled. "I've never been more sure about anything in my life. I want you to make love to me, Jerod. Please make love to me."

Her words seem to unleash him. His hands moved over the silk of her panties, quickly heating the material with the warmth of him. His fingers danced over her as his quickened breaths filled her ears.

She arched her hips up to meet his touch, and he took the opportunity to slide her panties down her legs and off. She plucked at his boxers, wanting him as naked as she was. He got out of them, and she immediately wrapped her fingers around his arousal. She tried to stroke him, but at the same time his fingers found the very core of her, and she couldn't contain the moan that escaped her.

All her energy coalesced at the place where he touched her as a tension began to build and build inside her. The tension broke as a climax shook through her, leaving her gasping and crying out his name.

He immediately moved between her thighs and hovered there, as if giving her one more chance to stop him. But the last thing she wanted was to halt the sweet, hot sensations he evoked in her.

She grabbed his buttocks and pulled him against her…into her.

When he was completely inside her, he froze and a low groan escaped him. His gaze caught hers, and in the depths of his eyes, she saw the same flames of desire that she knew burned in hers.

He began to stroke into her. Long and deep, he filled her up in a way she'd never been filled before. As the strokes became shorter and more frantic, she felt the throb of his climax approaching, and that caused her to fly over the edge once again.

He groaned and buried himself deep within her as they finished together. He half collapsed against her, both of them breathless.

He finally leaned up on his elbows and kissed her so softly, so sweetly that tears misted her eyes. He pushed aside the errant strand of her hair that always seemed to cling to the side of her face.

"That was amazing," he said softly and then rolled to the side.

"Yes, it was," she agreed, still boneless as she basked in the afterglow.

"I guess we should get up and get ready to go to sleep," he murmured, not moving.

"As soon as I can, I'll get up." She laughed. "Right now I'm not sure I can stand up."

"Same," he replied. "I love it when you smile,"

he said. He reached and traced her lips with his index finger. "You have a beautiful smile."

She looked at him in surprise. She wasn't used to compliments. "Thanks. Yours is pretty nice, too."

They smiled at each other, and Lily felt a peace rush through her that had been absent in her life. This man was her husband, and right now she felt like his wife. It was a wonderful feeling, but within minutes drowsiness overtook her.

"Okay, I've got to move now, otherwise I'll fall asleep and Caleb will find my naked, sleeping body in the morning."

He laughed. "We can't have that."

"And now I'll be right back." She slid out of the bed and grabbed her nightgown and panties from the floor and then went into the bathroom.

She stared at her reflection in the mirror. Her hair was tousled and her cheeks were flushed. Her eyes held a sparkling glow. She looked like a woman who had just been thoroughly loved. She felt like a woman who had thoroughly loved.

Making love with Jerod had been wonderful. He'd been gentle, and yet she'd felt the strength of his desire for her. She frowned and turned away from the mirror.

No matter what she felt at this moment, she knew better than to fool herself and believe it had been love that had brought them together tonight.

It had been an expression of the physical desire that had been building between them. And for him, he was probably hoping that she'd get pregnant and fulfill his desire for a child of his own.

Even though she'd looked into his eyes and had believed she'd seen all kinds of wonderful emotions, she needed to keep in mind what his ultimate goal was in being with her. He was saving her ranch, and in return he expected her to get pregnant and have his baby. So, of course he was eager to make love to her.

She cleaned up and pulled her panties and her nightgown back on. When she went back into the bedroom, Jerod was gone and she assumed he'd gone to the bathroom in the hallway.

She got back into bed and beneath the covers, and a couple minutes later he returned to the bedroom. He slid into bed and immediately pulled her close to him. She relaxed into him, ready to fall asleep in his arms whether they loved each other or not. Even if he didn't love her, she felt a closeness to him she couldn't deny, especially after what they'd just shared.

Sleepily she turned over, and he spooned her, his arm around her waist as he snuggled close against her back. "Lily," he whispered into her ear.

"Yes?" she whispered back.

"Now this day is a definite ten."

She smiled, and within minutes she was asleep.

She awakened the next morning to find herself alone in the bed. She glanced at the clock and was shocked to see it was almost nine. She'd forgotten to set her alarm the night before, and she had majorly overslept.

Her first thought was for Caleb, who was surely up by now and probably starving. She slid out of the bed, grabbed a robe and pulled it around her and then headed for the kitchen. She smelled both coffee and bacon.

Before she got there, she heard the deep rumble of Jerod's voice and then Caleb's laughter, and she immediately relaxed. She should have known that Jerod would take care of Caleb. That's what fathers did.

"Hey, Mom," Caleb greeted her with a bright smile. "Jerod was going to make eggs over easy, but he kept breaking the yolks, so we're eating his mistakes."

She smiled at Jerod, who stood in front of the stove and then looked back at her son. "And how many mistakes has he made?"

"So far six," Jerod admitted. "Caleb is eating three and I'm eating three."

"Maybe I should try to make me a couple," she said.

"No, you just sit and relax," Jerod replied. "On the last egg, I almost got it, and I'm determined to get one over-easy egg right. Caleb, why don't you pour your mother a cup of coffee?"

Her first instinct was to protest. Caleb had never poured her a cup of coffee before, and she knew how easy it would be for him to get burned if he spilled.

However, before she could say anything, Caleb jumped up from the table, and he looked so proud she decided to keep her mouth shut. She watched as he got down a cup, and then she held her breath as he carefully poured the coffee from the carafe into the awaiting cup.

As he delivered it to her, he gave her a big smile. "Just let me know when you're ready for a refill," he said.

"Thank you, Caleb." She returned his smile. Her son was growing up, and she realized she needed to let him do more in order to build both his independence and his confidence.

"Oh no, two more mistakes coming right up," Jerod said in dismay, making Caleb giggle. Jerod carried a plate with the two flattened eggs to her.

"They all taste the same," she replied. "And these look just fine for me."

As they ate, the topic of conversation was Caleb's horse. "Since it's Sunday, can you work with me today?" he asked Jerod.

"I think we can work something out once we finish our morning chores," Jerod replied.

"I already made my bed, and my room is clean," Caleb replied.

"That's great, but since Rod is off today, maybe you can help me for a little while in the barn," Jerod replied.

"Sure, I can do that." Caleb smiled at Jerod, and in her son's eyes Lily saw more than a little bit of hero worship going on. It wasn't going to take Caleb long to love Jerod with all his heart, and that scared her just a little bit.

She wanted to tell him not to fall too hard, that there was no real guarantee that Jerod would truly stick around. Unfortunately, Lily was going the way of her son. She was appalled to realize she was falling in love with her husband, and she couldn't forget that he had only married her as part of a business deal.

"Finally tonight I get to see the secretive science project," Jerod said Thursday morning as they were all eating breakfast.

"And we need to go over the schedule so everyone is on the same page," Lily said to both of them. "You'll pick up Caleb after school and bring him back here. I'm going to stay at school and help get things set up for the fair."

Jerod nodded. "I'll feed Caleb something for dinner, and then around six thirty I'm supposed to spray him down, throw some nice clothes on him, slick his hair back and be back at the school at seven."

"Hey, you aren't slicking my hair back in some kind of dorky style," Caleb protested, making both Lily and Jerod laugh.

"It was just a figure of speech, son," Jerod replied.

"Don't be figure of speeching about messing up my hair," Caleb replied and raised his hand to touch his thick brown hair.

"And then when the science fair is over, I need you and Caleb to come on home, and that night you can tuck him in because I'm staying late to help with all the cleanup," Lily said.

"I've got it down, Lily. You just focus on what you need to do, and Caleb and I will be just fine," Jerod assured her.

"Thanks," she replied with a smile.

They had made love a second time the night before, after they had gotten into the bed together. It had been slower and an exploration of each other. It had definitely been just as great as it had been the first time.

He found Lily to be an exciting, giving partner in the bedroom, but what would happen when she got pregnant? Once she fulfilled the terms of their "contract," would she expect that intimacy to stop?

Was she already pregnant? She wasn't on any

birth control, and there were plenty of teenagers who would be willing to attest that it only took one time for pregnancy to happen. Had it happened last night?

Excitement shot through his veins as he realized it was possible Lily could be carrying his child right now. This was what he had always wanted, what he'd dreamed about for so long. She had all the qualities he wanted in a mother to his children, and his dream of a real family felt like it was finally going to come true.

After breakfast she and Caleb left for the school, and Jerod headed for the barn, where Rod was already in the tack room oiling the equipment. "Good morning," he greeted Jerod.

"Back at you," Jerod replied.

The verdict was still out on Rod. He was a hard worker if given specific instructions, but if left on his own, he tended to do a whole lot of nothing.

Jerod didn't know if the man had been stealing from Lily or not, but now Jerod did the ordering and paying for supplies, so Rod would never have a chance to cheat or steal from Lily again.

Each evening Jerod left a list of chores he wanted done the next day. Aside from the chores that had to be done daily, Jerod had been working on cleaning out the barn. There was hay that had gone bad and needed to be out to make room for the hay Jerod needed to get in before winter. The barn showed years of neglect, and that needed to be changed.

"How is Lily doing?" Rod now asked. "I haven't seen her around for the last week."

"She's doing just fine. As long as we do our jobs, then she has less stress on her." Jerod always found it a bit disconcerting when Rod asked about Lily.

He assumed the man was just being friendly. However, Jerod hadn't lost track of the fact that somebody had left a mutilated doll and somebody had sent those boxers to create issues between them. Was Rod hoping Lily would divorce Jerod so she would once again be dependent on Rod?

The verdict was out. Thankfully he and Lily had been able to get past the boxer issue and hopefully whoever had left them now realized Lily and Jerod were a united front and intended to remain together.

The day passed quickly. Jerod worked in the barn through the morning, went in to eat lunch and then spent the afternoon riding among the herd, looking over their health and welfare.

At three thirty he drove into town to pick up Caleb from school. He waited only a few minutes before a flood of kids spilled out of the building. Some of them headed to awaiting parents' vehicles while others loaded up in one of the three buses that were parked in front.

He spied Caleb and waved out the window. Caleb ran toward his truck with a bright smile on his face.

"How was school today?" he asked once Caleb was in the truck and they were headed back home.

"It was good," Caleb replied. "I'm just excited about tonight. After we have the official science fair stuff, there is going to be cupcakes and drinks."

Jerod laughed. "If there are cupcakes involved, it has to be a good night, right?"

"Right. It's going to be fun to see all the projects, but I think mine and Benny's is the best. We've really worked hard on it."

"It's going to be fun for me to see yours," Jerod replied. "And I've noticed that you've been really good about controlling your anger."

Caleb released a deep sigh. "I was just so mad that my dad didn't stick around to be with me, but I'm not so mad anymore. Besides, I think you're a better father than he would have been."

Jerod's heart squeezed tight, and love for this fatherless boy filled him. "I'm glad you feel that way about me," he finally managed to say.

"The only thing I worry about now is if you're going to stay forever with me and my mom," Caleb said.

"That's my plan, and you don't need to worry

about that. All I want you to do is be a nine-year-old boy who isn't worried about any grown-up issues."

"That's my plan," Caleb parroted back to him with a grin.

They had hot dogs, and Jerod opened up a can of beans for dinner. As they ate the two talked about what they each saw for their future, what Jerod had experienced in his past and the dangers of drugs and alcohol.

It was a good talk between two males, bonding moments that Jerod knew were good for Caleb and himself. It was obvious Caleb was hungry for this kind of male interaction and support.

After eating, they both cleaned up to get ready for the science fair. Caleb put on his suit without Jerod prompting him, and Jerod wore a pair of black slacks with a gray dress shirt.

They both pulled on jackets, and Jerod grabbed Lily's coat from the hall closet to take to the school. The day had turned blustery and cold, and he knew she'd appreciate her coat later in the evening when she finally headed back home.

Caleb could scarcely sit still in the passenger seat as Jerod drove to the school. He bounced and wiggled in obvious excitement. "I hope you like my project. Me and Benny spent a lot of hours working on it. We had to study and make stuff for it." Caleb looked at him for a long moment. "I hope when you see it you're proud of me."

The longing in Caleb's voice once again tugged at Jerod's heartstrings. "As long as you did your best, then I'm very proud of you."

Caleb nodded and then sat back in the seat as if satisfied with Jerod's response.

The elementary school was a one-level brick building. Tonight the whole parking lot was full of the cars and trucks of the parents who'd come to see their students' work.

They wound up having to park on a side street a half a block away. The cold front that had moved in brought with it a nip of winter fast approaching. They hurried toward the school, spurred not so much by the cold but rather by Caleb's excitement.

"Hey," Jerod yelled at Caleb as he raced across the street ahead of him. When Jerod caught up with him, he took Caleb by the arm. "Caleb, you don't ever run across a street without stopping and looking both ways. You could get seriously hurt that way."

"I'm sorry. Please don't be mad at me," Caleb replied, his blue eyes pleading. "I was just too excited."

"I'm not mad at you, but what you did was very dangerous, and I don't want anything bad to happen to you," Jerod explained.

Caleb nodded. "I kind of like it that you yelled at me. That's something a dad would do. I want you to yell at me when I do something wrong."

Jerod threw his arm around Caleb's shoulder. "Come on, let's get inside and find your mom."

The science fair was set up in the gym, with each grade's offerings in different areas of the big room. It was noisy and chaotic, but everyone had smiles on their faces.

They found the fourth-grade section, but before they could get to Caleb's project, Maggie Rogers, one of Lily's school friends, snagged them to see the project her son, Anthony, and his partner had done. It was a study on earthworms and their benefits.

Before they could get away from Maggie, Krista grabbed Jerod by the arm to show him and Caleb her son Henry's project. It was labeled "Talking to Plants," and as Jerod and Caleb stood listening to Krista explain all about it, he found himself impatient to get to Caleb and Benny's offering.

"Are you trying to steal my husband?" Lily's light voice was a welcome relief as she came up behind them.

"Absolutely," Krista replied with a laugh.

Jerod turned around to greet his wife. He'd forgotten how lovely she'd looked at breakfast that morning, and she was just as lovely tonight. The black slacks she wore showcased her long, slender legs, and the pale pink blouse enhanced her blue eyes and pretty, clear complexion.

"Hi, wife," he said to her. He could tell the greeting both surprised and pleased her.

"Hi, husband," she replied with a bright smile.

"You two are nauseating," Krista said.

Lily laughed. "We're leaving." She placed her hands on Caleb's shoulders. "I'm eager for Jerod to see Caleb and Benny's project."

"And I'm eager to see it, too," Jerod replied.

As they walked away from Krista, Jerod gave her the coat he had brought from home. "It's gotten cold, so I thought you might need this later when you leave."

"Thank you, that was very thoughtful. You both look very nice," Lily said as she led them down the aisle of tables to the very end.

"Jerod helped me with my tie," Caleb said. He practically danced in front of a display board that held the title "All About Earthquakes." The board was carefully printed with facts about earthquakes and in particular earthquakes in Oklahoma. In front of the poster board was a homemade seismograph and a tower of blocks with strings attached to the blocks on the bottom level.

"This is how earthquakes happen," Caleb said with self-importance. He pulled on the strings to move the lower blocks, mimicking the way the earth's plates shifted.

"Caleb, this is awesome," Jerod said. "I can see how much thought and work you put in this, and as far as I'm concerned you should definitely win a blue ribbon for it."

Caleb's shoulders shot back, and his eyes lit with pride. "Thanks. Benny and I wanted to make it as good as we could."

"All your hard work definitely shows," Jerod replied.

Within minutes people began to walk through the aisles, looking at all the projects. Lily and Jerod watched as Caleb and Benny greeted the people who stopped to see theirs. Jerod felt like a proud father as he saw the friendly poise Caleb showed to each person.

"I'm assigned to walk around and look for any problems or issues," Lily said after a few minutes.

"Go do your job. Caleb and I will be just fine here," he assured her.

"I'll check in with you two later," she replied.

For the next hour, Jerod stood behind the table and watched the people come and go by the table. "Here comes my teacher," Caleb said as an attractive middle-aged blonde approached. Jerod recognized her from around town, but he didn't know her personally.

"Hi, Mrs. Burwell," Caleb greeted her.

"Hello, Caleb." She looked at Jerod and then back at Caleb. "And who do you have here with you?"

Caleb linked his arm through Jerod's. "This

is Jerod…he's my new dad." Caleb smiled up at him with such pride, such love that it momentarily rendered Jerod speechless.

The weight of Caleb's love both buoyed in his heart and hung heavy on his shoulders. He knew that if for any reason this marriage didn't work out between him and Lily, Caleb would be destroyed by what he'd perceive as another man rejecting him and walking out of his life.

It had been a wonderful evening. Caleb and Benny had won first place in their grade level and had celebrated by eating two cupcakes each and high-fiving each other until their hands were red.

Lily was beyond proud and had also been pleased by how attentive Jerod had been to Caleb and to her. It had been so thoughtful of him to bring her the winter coat. Did it mean he was falling in love with her? No. It was just more proof that he was a caring man.

However, right now as she helped Carol and Brad and two other teachers clear up the last of the mess in the gymnasium, she was just exhausted and eager to get home.

"Thank God we don't have to clean up the floors," Brad said.

Lily looked around. The floor was littered with pieces of projects, spilled fruit drinks and fallen cupcakes. "I feel sorry for Roger. He has his work cut out for him tonight."

Roger Tatum was the school janitor, who would come in later this evening to get the floors polished and the bathrooms cleaned up before morning, when a new school day began.

There were only half a dozen tables and ten or twelve chairs left to pick up. Brad and the two other teachers tackled the tables, and Lily and Carol finished up putting the chairs away in a large closet just off the gym.

Finally everything was done, and the minute it was, everyone else scooted out of the building while Lily went back to her classroom to retrieve her coat.

Thankfully, tomorrow was Friday, so she only had one more day to get through before she'd have the weekend to rest and relax. She pulled on her coat and then headed for the school's front door.

When she stepped outside, she pulled her coat collar closer around her neck. The temperature was definitely chillier tonight than it had been this morning when she'd left for work. She was definitely grateful for her coat.

Her truck was the only vehicle left in the parking lot, and as she headed toward it, she hit her key fob to unlock it and then dropped the fob back into her purse.

She welcomed the quiet of the night after the

hours of noise and barely controlled chaos. She was at her truck door when she sensed somebody behind her. She whirled around in time to see a figure dressed all in black and wearing a ski mask.

She had only a moment to process it when the person raised a big, sharp knife. The utter shock, the horror and confusion of what was happening momentarily froze Lily in place.

The inertia snapped, and Lily managed to jump to the left. The knife sank into her shoulder and then was pulled out. If she hadn't moved, the knife would have stabbed her in the chest.

Shock, along with excruciating pain, shot through her. Once again the attacker came after her, obviously trying to stab her in the chest. But Lily used her purse as a shield, deflecting several of the attempts.

Who was this person? Why was this happening? A thousand questions flew frantically through Lily's mind as the knife kept coming. She screamed as the knife ripped through her coat and dug into her ribs.

Get away, her brain screamed in alarm as tears blurred her vision. *Get into the truck and lock the doors.* If she didn't manage to get into the truck, then eventually the attacker was going to stab her to death. She could already feel the trickle of blood from the wounds she'd already received.

But in order to get into the truck, she'd have to

turn her back on the attacker. She sidestepped and attempted to pull the truck door open, but the assailant leaned into it in an effort to keep Lily out. The door slammed shut.

The knife pierced Lily again, this time in her arm. She had to get in her vehicle, otherwise the attacker was going to keep stabbing and slashing until Lily was dead.

She screamed once again as she lost her footing and nearly fell. If she hit the ground and the person managed to get on top of her, Lily knew she'd be dead within minutes.

They struggled with the truck door, and with a roar of pure survival need and adrenaline, Lily shoved the door open, got inside and then locked the truck. She leaned her head against the steering wheel, her breath coming in deep, ragged pants.

She had no idea how badly she was hurt. She knew she was bleeding from several places. She raised her head and frantically searched around the area, but she saw nobody. The attacker was gone, apparently swallowed up by the night.

She put her head back down on the steering wheel and began to cry again as she thought of what had just happened...what might have happened if she hadn't successfully gotten into the truck. Somebody had just tried to kill her. Her brain couldn't even wrap around the very idea.

As minutes ticked by and the adrenaline began

to ebb away, she was too weak, too shaken to even start the truck and try to drive. She needed help. She finally leaned on the horn, hoping the noise would get somebody's attention.

She jumped with renewed terror as a knock sounded on her window. She raised up and snapped her head around to see who it was. It was Roger, the school janitor. She released a deep sob as she rolled down her window. "Roger, call Dillon. I—I've been attacked. I—I've been stabbed."

Roger's eyes widened as he dug his cell phone out of his pocket. He placed the call to the chief of police and also told Dillon to send an ambulance. "Lily, is there anything else I can do for you?" he asked worriedly. "There's a first aid kit in the school. But I'm not sure if there's anything more useful than small bandages in there."

"Thanks, but I'm okay here until the ambulance comes. Just please stay with me until Dillon gets here," she replied. Pain seared through each wound on her body. Who had done this to her and why? God, the attacker had wanted to kill her and had almost succeeded. Why was this happening? Who would want her dead?

"Do you want me to call Jerod for you?" Roger asked.

"No, I'll call him." She was torn. Jerod was at home with Caleb, and that's where he belonged. She didn't want him to yank her son out of bed and frighten him with what had just happened to her. Yet she knew if she didn't get home soon, then Jerod would worry about where she was.

She saw the swirl of red lights down the street and knew Dillon was approaching. "Thank you, Roger, for staying with me."

"I wish I could have done more for you, Lily," he replied worriedly.

She forced a smile through her tears. "I just appreciate you calling for help."

By that time Dillon had pulled up, along with two other patrol cars and an ambulance. Dillon stepped out of his car and hurried over to the side of her truck. "Lily, what's going on?"

"Somebody attacked me, Dillon. I—I've been stabbed. Somebody came up to me at the truck and started stabbing me." She began to cry again from pain and the residual sheer terror of the attack.

"Where are you hurt?" Dillon asked urgently. He opened the truck door and looked at her in worried concern.

"My shoulder…and in my ribs…and I don't know where else." She felt like she was just now climbing out of her shock, and her entire body hurt.

Dillon motioned the men in the ambulance to bring the stretcher. "Can you tell me anything about the attacker?"

"No, except whoever it was, was dressed all in black and wore a ski mask."

When the stretcher was right next to the truck, one of the paramedics helped her out of the truck and onto the stretcher. "Lily, I'll meet you at the hospital and get the particulars from you once you've been treated," Dillon said.

Tears began falling again as they put her into the ambulance and she saw the blood on her coat. They removed the coat and cut off her blouse, exposing the wounds not only on her shoulder and her stomach, but also a deep slash on her arm.

The paramedics put in an IV and cleaned the wounds and then rushed her to the hospital and the emergency room. The next hour went by in a blur. The doctor put fifteen stitches in her shoulder and ten in her arm. Thankfully the wound to her stomach had missed all her vital organs and required no stitches.

She was now clad in a hospital gown because her blouse had been ruined. Her IV had finally been removed, and all she wanted to do was go home.

When the doctor left her little cubicle, she grabbed her phone and saw that Jerod had called her several times. She dialed him, and he answered on the first ring. "Lily, where are you? I've been worried sick about you," he said.

"First of all, I want to let you know I'm okay.

Somebody attacked me when I was leaving the school. I'm at the hospital now and I still need to speak with Dillon, but after that I'll be home." She tried to sound strong even though she wanted to cry once again.

"What do you mean you were attacked?"

"Somebody stabbed me."

"Wh-who? Who did it?" His worry and his outrage were both evident in his voice.

"I don't know who it was," she replied. "I'll explain more when I get home, but I just wanted to let you know what was going on." She looked up as Dillon came into the small room. "Dillon is here with me now. I'll be home later."

Before Jerod could say anything more, she hung up and looked at the dark-haired lawman. "You doing okay?" he asked as he sat in the chair next to the hospital bed.

"I'll be a lot better once I get home and can take one of the pain pills the doctor prescribed for me."

"He didn't give you anything yet?"

"No, I wanted to be completely clearheaded when I spoke to you, and besides, I need to drive myself home when we're finished."

"So, tell me exactly what happened," he asked. He pulled out his phone and set it on the table in front of her. "Do I have permission to tape you?"

"Of course. So, you know the science fair was tonight," she began. She told him about staying late to help with the cleanup and that she'd been the last one to leave the school.

"By the time I left, my truck was the only vehicle in the parking lot. I got to the side of my truck and sensed somebody behind me, and then the person started stabbing me."

She went through everything that had happened…about fighting to get the truck door open, about the person being in a frenzy as the stabbing continued, and finally the fact that she had managed to get in to truck until Roger had found her.

As she spoke, she felt as if she'd gone ten rounds with a heavyweight champion. Her entire body hurt, and she didn't even want to think about all the stitches she'd received.

"Okay, now I have some questions," Dillon said. "You said you didn't know the attacker. Can you give me a general description?"

She shook her head. "Not really. It was so dark out, and the person was dressed all in black and wore a ski mask."

"What about size? Was the person short or tall? Heavyset or thin?"

She looked at him helplessly. "It was so dark," she said, knowing she was repeating herself. "I'm sorry, Dillon. Everything happened so fast." She frowned, the gesture making her realize her head ached.

"All I was focused on was the knife and trying to get away. I can't even tell you what size the person was. The only thing I know for sure is that the attacker wanted me dead."

"Who were the people who left the school right before you did?" Dillon asked.

She told him the names of the people.

"But you didn't see any cars in the parking lot when you left," Dillon replied.

"None. My truck was the only vehicle." Lily shifted in the bed, the pain from her wounds getting worse rather than better. "Who would want me dead, Dillon? Why did this happen to me?"

"I don't know, Lily, but I'm going to do everything in my power to find out. My men are at the school right now looking for any evidence that might lead to an arrest. In the meantime the doctor told me you're free to go, and so whenever you're ready, I'll take you back to your truck and then follow you home unless you want to make other arrangements."

She'd love to make other arrangements. She'd love to just magically be transported into her bed and into Jerod's arms. But that wasn't going to happen. "I'm ready for you to take me to my truck."

Dillon helped her out of the bed. "Hopefully nobody will mind if I wear the hospital gown home and bring it back tomorrow," she said.

"I'm sure that will be fine," Dillon replied and

then frowned. "Are you sure you're going to be able to drive home?"

She felt nauseous and shaky and like she was in a nightmare she couldn't escape, but she nodded affirmatively to Dillon. She had no choice but to drive herself home. She refused to call Jerod and disrupt Caleb's sleep.

"As long as you follow me home," she said. "I don't want anything else bad happening tonight."

"Trust me, I'll make sure you get home safely." Dillon's dark eyes burned with determination.

The ride from the hospital to the school was a quiet one. The doctor had given Lily a couple of pain pills until somebody could get to the pharmacy the next day to pick up a prescription. All she could think about was taking a pill and getting into bed. Maybe when she woke up tomorrow, she'd find out this had all been a bad dream.

They reached her truck. The other officers were still at the school, their flashlights beaming brightly through the darkness of the night. Their presence reassured her. Maybe they would find a clue that would identify the attacker. God, she needed that to happen. She needed to know who hated her enough to want her dead.

Once she was alone in her truck with Dillon following right behind her, she began to weep once again. Who had done this to her? Who had tried to stab her to death? And why?

Who had hidden out in the dark and then attacked her with the intention of killing her? The whole thing seemed so...so crazy.

She couldn't think of anyone who might want to harm her. She'd never had cross words with anyone. Was the attacker the same person who had left the bride doll? The boxers? If so, then the person had escalated things to a terrifying and dangerous level.

When they reached her house, she pulled up and parked. Dillon parked behind her and jumped out of his car and came to her door. "I'll walk you to the door," he said. "And then I'll be by sometime tomorrow afternoon to check in with you and let you know how the investigation is progressing."

"Thank you, Dillon." She eased out of the truck, but before they reached the front door, it flew open and Jerod stepped out on the porch.

"Lily," he said and rushed to her side. "What happened?" He started to wrap his arms around her, but she stopped him.

"Please...be careful. I have stitches in my arm and shoulder," she said and began to cry.

Dillon quickly related to Jerod a shortened version of what had happened. "I'll be by tomorrow, but in the meantime, if you think of anything that might be helpful in identifying the person, don't hesitate to call me." With these words, he turned and left.

Jerod walked her through the front door, and she immediately headed down the hallway toward the bedroom. She knew he'd have questions, but she was in pain and exhausted.

Once they reached the bedroom, she sank down on the edge of the bed. Gingerly Jerod sat next to her. "What can I do to help?" he asked.

"The doctor gave me some pain pills. Would you mind getting me a glass of water so I can take one?"

"Of course." He immediately got up and headed into the kitchen.

While he was gone, she took off her slacks and then sat down on the bed still wearing the hospital gown. Jerod returned to the room with a glass of water.

She pulled her purse up next to her, reached inside and retrieved the envelope that contained three pain pills. She took the pill, handed him back the glass and then eased down in the bed.

Jerod sat down on the edge and gazed at her. In his dark eyes she saw compassion along with a hot burn of anger. He picked up the arm that had the stitches. "Where else are you hurt?" His voice was low and held a controlled outrage.

"My shoulder and my stomach," she replied. "Jerod, the attacker tried to kill me. The knife just kept stabbing and stabbing at me." A shiver raced up her spine.

"We're going to find out who did this, Lily." His voice held an edge of steel. "I swear, we're going to get this person, and whoever it is better hope that Dillion gets them before I do."

"Right now I just want to go to sleep," she replied. Any lingering adrenaline had left her, and the pill was already taking the edges off her pain. She was absolutely exhausted by the whole ordeal.

Jerod turned off the light and got into the bed. "I want to hold you, Lily, but I also don't want to hurt you."

"I appreciate the thought, but I'm also afraid you'll hurt me. I think it's best if we just go to sleep." She closed her eyes, and instantly her mind began to take her to dark places. Somebody wanted her dead, which could only mean that somebody wanted her out of Jerod's life permanently.

Was Jerod being completely honest about everything? Or did he have a secret lover who wanted Lily out of the picture? Now that Lily and Jerod were married, if anything happened to her, he would be her beneficiary and would get the ranch. Had that been his scheme the whole time?

Was he in on a plot to have her murdered?

Dear God, who could she really trust?

Chapter 8

Lily awoke to the sun shining in her bedroom window. She was alone in the bed with only pain as her bedmate. Her stab wounds hurt, but the hurt didn't stop there. Every muscle in her body ached as if she'd been beaten up in her sleep by night demons.

Looking at the clock on the nightstand, she was vaguely surprised to see it was almost ten o'clock. She had no idea what time she had gotten home the night before—all she knew was that it had been late.

She hoped somebody had contacted the school to let them know she wouldn't be in today. She assumed Jerod had seen to it that Caleb had had breakfast and had gotten to school earlier.

Jerod.

As she stared up at the ceiling, all her dark thoughts about her husband rushed back to her mind. She didn't want to believe that Jerod had had anything to do with the attack on her. She definitely didn't want to believe he'd had such a terrible ulterior motive for marrying her. But it was so difficult to know whom to trust.

She finally pulled herself out of bed and into the bathroom. She took off the hospital gown and tossed it into the laundry basket and then stared at herself in the mirror.

The stitches looked huge against her pale skin, and as she remembered the attack, a cold chill shivered up her spine. If she hadn't managed to get inside her truck, she would have been killed. There was no doubt about it in her mind. Somebody would have found her cold, dead body next to her truck.

She took a warm washcloth and washed herself off and then pulled on a fresh pair of pink and white polka-dotted flannel pajama pants and matching top. There was no point in getting dressed. She had absolutely no intention of leaving the house today.

When she was finished dressing, she headed for the kitchen, where she found Jerod seated at the table and what looked and smelled like fresh coffee in the pot.

He jumped out of his chair at the sight of her. "Lily…sit and I'll get you a cup of coffee." She sank down at the table. "How are you feeling this morning?"

"Like I got run over by a huge truck that had very sharp teeth," she replied. He set her coffee cup before her, and she wrapped her fingers around its warmth. However, she had an icy chill deep inside her that no amount of external heat would be able to reach.

"What can I do to help you?" He returned to the table and looked at her in concern. Was he concerned because she'd been attacked or was he sorry that she'd survived the attack?

She broke eye contact with him and instead stared down into her coffee. "If you wouldn't mind, maybe you could go into town later and pick up my prescriptions. I think I have two…for pain and an antibiotic."

"Of course I'll take care of that," he replied. "I called Mr. Cook early this morning to let him know you wouldn't be in for work." John Cook was the principal at the school. "And I also arranged for Krista to take Caleb to and from school today."

"Thank you for all of that." She took a sip of coffee and then looked at him again. "Did you say anything about all this to Caleb this morning?" Dear God, she wanted to protect her son from this evil, but she wasn't sure she could considering her current physical condition.

"I told him that somebody attacked you last night, but I also told him we think the person was trying to rob you," he replied. "I hope I didn't overstep."

"No…we had to tell him something," she replied. "I suppose that was as good as anything. And you got him to school this morning?"

"Actually, Krista came and got him as a favor. She was very worried about you after she found out what happened."

"That's right, you already told me she took Caleb to school." Lily rubbed the center of her forehead as if she could unscramble her mind. "Did you tell her it was a robbery attempt?" she asked.

"No, I only told her that you'd been attacked. You and I both know this wasn't a robbery attempt. Lily, I'm so angry that somebody did this to you. I'm especially ticked off that I wasn't there to protect you." His eyes were dark with anger, and she desperately wanted to believe him, but all her doubts rushed to the forefront and she couldn't ignore them anymore.

She drew in a deep breath and held his gaze.

"Jerod, did you marry me to get my ranch?" she asked. "And am I now in your way?"

His eyes sparked with a new anger and disbelief. He jerked back in his chair as if she'd physically slapped him. "What are you talking about? Lily, what in the hell is going on in that pretty head of yours?" His gaze searched her features.

She should have never said anything. She really didn't want and didn't feel strong enough to open up this particular can of worms, but she hadn't been able to help herself.

Tears burned at her eyes, and once again she stared down into her coffee cup. "I just… I've just been trying to figure out why this is happening to me."

"And you're somehow figuring out that I had something to do with the attack on you?" His voice held incredulity. "In what world would that happen? Lily, please look at me and tell me what's going on in your head."

She released another deep breath and then looked back up at him. "Last night when I was in bed, my mind struggled to make sense of everything. One of the things I thought about was that maybe…uh…maybe you secretly have a girlfriend…" Her voice trailed off as he leaned forward.

"And?"

Her heart beat with anxiety, and her wounds

on her arm and shoulder burned. "And I thought maybe you married me and then if I die you'd get the ranch because we're married and then you and your girlfriend could live here together." The words blurted out of her on a rush.

He stared at her and his mouth opened…then closed, as if he had no words. He finally opened his mouth once again. "Jeez, Lily, how could you even have that thought in your brain?"

He searched her features as if somehow trying to see inside her brain. "If I wanted a ranch, it would have been much easier to just go buy one. I have the money to get my own place. If you would feel better about things, then let's get a lawyer to draw up an agreement that no matter what happens between us, this ranch belongs to you, and after your death it will go to whoever you want it to."

He drew in a deep breath and released it slowly. "Lily, I married you because I admired the kind of woman you are. You are the kind of woman I'd like to have a family with. I married you because I thought we could help each other achieve what each of us most wanted in life."

He got up out of the chair and knelt next to hers. "Lily, have you ever heard anything about me that would make you believe I'm a potential murderer? Have you ever heard that I'm dishonest or have dishonored any woman, that I'm in any way the kind of monster you're talking about?"

He pulled her hand into his. "Believe me, Lily, you are my wife, and I care about you, not this ranch. We're on notice now that somebody is after you. From this day on, I will defend you against anyone who tries to harm you with my very life. My number-one goal is to keep you safe." He squeezed her hand as if to emphasize his words.

His gaze now telegraphed to her a grave concern, along with a grim determination, and all she felt was utter confusion. She had never, ever heard a bad word about Jerod Steen in town or anywhere else.

He was definitely right that there was an easier way for him to get a ranch rather than to come up with a complex plot to kill her and take her land by some kind of a sick default.

"As far as getting your medication from the pharmacy, I can do a drive-through, but I really don't want to leave you here alone. Can you ride with me?"

She nodded as a new chill swept through her. She hadn't thought about being in danger here in her home. But somebody could break in, knowing she was here alone and banged up. She'd make an easy victim right now because, at the moment, physically she didn't think she'd be able to fight off a butterfly.

Jerod got up from the table. "Now, what would you like for breakfast?"

"I'm really not hungry."

He frowned. "You should eat a little something with the pills you're taking. How about a piece of buttered toast?"

Even though she wasn't a bit hungry, she knew he was right about getting a little something in her stomach. "Okay."

She watched as he got out the bread and butter. Logically, she knew Jerod was a good man. Her brain rejected the idea that he was a liar, a cheater and had planned to conspire to murder her. She was just so frightened. And she had no idea who had been the attacker the night before.

He set the toast in front of her and then once again sat at the table. "Thanks. At least before the attack it had been a wonderful night," she said, desperate to change the subject.

Jerod smiled. "I practically had to hog-tie Caleb to get him into bed last night because he was so excited from their win."

She couldn't help but smile as she thought of her son. "Even if he hadn't won, I was so proud of him and the way he interacted with everyone who came to their table."

"I was, too. He introduced me to his teacher as his new dad."

"I guess I'm not surprised by that. I've seen

how close he's gotten to you. I've also noticed that the anger inside him seems to have subsided."

She paused and took a drink of her coffee. "I... I just hope he doesn't get hurt...that the two of us don't somehow disappoint him."

"I was so honored, so touched when he said that to his teacher. Caleb wants what I've wanted all my life—a real family with a mother and a father to love and support him. And we need to stay together and remain strong so we don't ever disappoint him." Once again his eyes darkened. "I thought that's what we were doing until you told me what you'd been thinking about me."

Her cheeks flushed with warmth. "I can't help where my thoughts took me last night. Jerod, I'm really scared."

His hand reached out and covered one of hers. "Lily, I can't imagine what you went through last night. When I think about it, it makes me sick. It chills my blood and it makes me angry as hell."

"If you hadn't brought me my winter coat and if I hadn't had it on, I'd probably be dead. At least the thickness of the coat deflected some of the worst of the damage."

"Thank God for that. All I want you to know, Lily, is that I'm on your side," he said. He drew his hand back. "Now eat your toast so you don't get a stomachache from your medication."

He got up from the table and left the kitchen.

By the time Lily had eaten the toast and put the small plate in the dishwasher, Jerod had returned to the kitchen, this time with a holster and gun around his waist.

"I thought maybe we could go ahead and get your medicine this morning so you can get back and just rest," he said. "I know you probably don't feel like getting out, but you really need to take the ride with me. I don't want to leave you here alone."

She nodded. "I'm not getting dressed. If we're doing the drive-through at the pharmacy, I don't intend to get out and have anyone see me."

"That's fine with me," he replied and then offered her a grin. "Although you look very cute and cuddly in those pink polka dots."

To her surprise a laugh escaped her. "Well, that is something," she replied.

Fifteen minutes later they were in Jerod's truck and headed into town. Lily was surprised by the edge of fear that rose up in her in being outside the safety of her home.

Jerod shot her a quick glance. "Doing okay?"

"Just a little bit nervous," she replied.

"Nobody is going to hurt you, Lily, not while I'm with you."

"Rationally I believe that, but emotionally I'm still all over the place."

"I'm sure that's normal considering what you

went through last night," he replied. "You went through a terrible ordeal, and it's going to take some time for you to process all of it. You know whenever you need to talk about what's happened or what is happening, you can always talk to me."

He looked at her again, and in his eyes she saw a wealth of caring. How was it possible to entertain suspicions about a man she was falling in love with? Her brain had obviously been scrambled from the attack. She still felt like she was in a bit of shock over what had happened to her.

They got her prescriptions, and when they got home she took her medicine and decided to stretch out on the sofa and rest. "Shouldn't you be working on things outside?" she asked Jerod as he sat in the chair across from the sofa.

"I called Rod, and he's got a handle on everything that needs to be done for the next couple of days. When you get back to work, then I'll get back to work outside. Don't worry about anything, Lily. I've got it all covered."

She closed her eyes as a deep exhaustion tugged at her. She felt so tired, and the pain gnawed at her. Jerod covered her with a light, fuzzy blanket from the closet, and she snuggled beneath it, still trying to fight off the icy chill inside her.

She fell asleep and into a nightmare where she was being chased down a dark street. She ran as fast as she could, her breath coming in deep pants as she tried to outrun whoever was chasing her. She could hear the footsteps echoing behind her, getting closer and closer. In her heart she knew who was chasing her.

It was death.

"I just can't believe this happened to you," Krista said to Lily. She'd brought Caleb home from school and now sat in the living room with Lily. Henry and Caleb were in Caleb's room while Jerod was in the kitchen getting ready to cook dinner.

As he formed hamburger into patties, he could hear the two women talking. "Carol is going to bring you a casserole tomorrow," Krista said. "I'd offer to bring you one, but you know I don't cook."

"I'd be afraid to eat any casserole you made," Lily replied with a laugh.

It was good to hear her laugh with her friend. His and her morning conversation had been pretty grim. She'd made him angry. The fact that she had doubted him and his intentions had definitely ticked him off, and if he was honest with himself, he'd been hurt.

But he believed it wasn't so much about him as much as it was about her terror. And that terror was what had her mistrusting everyone around her, including him. All he could do was prove with every action he took that he was on her side.

He'd had to wake her from a nightmare earlier. She'd fallen asleep on the sofa, and the next thing he knew, she was screaming and thrashing about. He'd gently touched her to awaken her, and she had come up and into his arms sobbing and shaking.

He knew what a strong woman Lily was, and it broke his heart to see her so frightened and fragile.

He now placed the patties in a skillet and then went to the refrigerator to pull out ingredients for a salad. He didn't know how to cook much, but he could fry up some burgers, and he knew how much Lily liked salad.

He'd thought they'd been on such a good path before all this had happened. They had been enjoying each other's company, and their intimacy had seemed natural and good. He'd been excited about his relationship with Caleb and what he'd believed he'd been building with Lily.

And she didn't trust him.

He shoved this thought out of his head. He had to get over it. She couldn't help the way she felt right now. In any case, he was glad Krista had stopped by to not only bring Caleb home from school but also to lift Lily's spirits.

Krista and Henry stayed for another hour or so, and by the time they left, Jerod had dinner on the table. He'd smothered the hamburger patties with canned tomato sauce and had added in some seasoning and then topped each of them with mozzarella cheese. He'd also made some garlic bread on the side.

"This looks delicious," Lily said and looked at him in surprise.

"I used my imagination a bit, so I hope it tastes as good as it looks," he replied.

"I'm sure it's going to be awesome," Caleb said with a look of confidence at Jerod.

"Then maybe you should taste it before your mom and I do," Jerod suggested.

"Okay." Caleb cut a piece of the hamburger patty and popped it into his mouth. He chewed a couple of times and then his eyes widened, he grabbed his throat and fell off his chair.

"Okay, you little comedian," Jerod said with a laugh.

Caleb giggled and got back in his chair. "Actually, Mom, it's really good."

"I didn't know you could cook anything other than egg mistakes," she said to him.

He laughed. "I still have a few tricks up my sleeves when it comes to cooking."

"Like what?" Caleb asked.

"Oh, I can grill a really good steak and make a good pot of chili," he replied.

"Hmm, Caleb and I love chili," Lily replied.

"Then maybe tomorrow night I'll make a big

pot of it," he said. He was grateful to see Lily a little more relaxed this evening.

Their good moods lasted through the meal, and then they all settled back into the living room, Lily stretched out on the sofa, Jerod in the chair and Caleb seated on the floor.

"Is Mr. Bowie going to catch the man who hurt you, Mom?" Caleb asked.

"I'm sure he will. That's what the police do… they catch the bad guys," she replied. "But I don't want to talk about that tonight. Did I ever tell you about the time one of my students tried to tell me he didn't have his homework because his baby sister ate it?"

"So what happened?" Caleb asked.

"He told me they had to go to the hospital and cut open her stomach to get it out, but it was too yucky to turn in from being in her stomach with her formula."

"That sounds like a pretty tall tale to me," Caleb said with a laugh.

"Did you believe him?" Caleb asked.

"No, son. I didn't," she replied with a laugh. "But I should have given him an A for his story-telling skills."

"Do you have any funny stories from when you were younger?" Caleb asked Jerod.

"Yes, tell us some funny stories, Jerod," Lily said. "I feel like being entertained tonight."

"When all the cowboys at the Holiday Ranch were younger, we used to play pranks on each other all the time," Jerod said. He allowed his mind to drift back in time and began to talk about some of the funniest things they'd done to each other when they'd all been nothing but boys.

He told them about throwing smoke bombs into the bathrooms of unsuspecting victims, about putting smelly things beneath bed pillows and other silly things.

The more Caleb and Lily laughed, the sillier his stories became. He loved to see Lily laugh. Her pretty eyes sparkled, and all the worried lines on her face disappeared. Then Lily began sharing more student funnies, and before they knew it, it was Caleb's bedtime.

While he showered, Caleb and Lily continued to talk about funny things. Jerod was just grateful to see her smile, to hear her laugh despite what had happened to her and the injuries she'd sustained.

"I guess laughter is the best medicine," she said once Caleb was in bed and the two of them were alone once again.

"I love the sound of your laughter," he replied. "I'd love to hear it every day of my life."

Her cheeks turned a pretty pink. "Jerod… about the conversation I had with you earlier this morning…"

"It's already forgotten," he replied and gave her a reassuring smile. "We just need to move forward, Lily."

She opened her mouth to respond, but a knock on the door interrupted her. Jerod grabbed his gun from the end table next to where he had been sitting. He held it before him and then opened the door.

He immediately dropped the gun barrel to point at the floor as Dillon greeted him. "Come on in," Jerod said and opened the door wider to allow the lawman inside.

Any levity Jerod might have felt before disappeared as he saw the grim lines of Dillon's face. "Good evening, Lily," Dillon said.

Lily rose up and swung her legs over the edge of the sofa so she was sitting up. "Hi, Dillon."

"I told you I'd come by today and check in with both of you. Lily, how are you doing?"

"I'm still in some pain, but I feel a little better this evening," she replied.

"She's frightened, Dillon. And I'm frightened for her," Jerod said and gestured Dillon into the chair. He then sat on the sofa next to Lily.

"I certainly understand your fear given what happened," Dillon replied.

"So, what do you have for us?" Jerod asked.

"Unfortunately, not much." Dillon frowned, creating a deep crease across his forehead. "My men went over the area in and around the school parking lot, but we found nothing of evidentiary value there. I've also been unable to find any witnesses to the attack."

"That doesn't surprise me," Lily said. "As far as I know, we were the only two people anywhere around."

Jerod reached over and took her hand in his. Every time he thought of her all alone in the parking lot with a knife-wielding attacker, he wanted to hurt someone. He wanted to find the perpetrator and beat them within an inch of their lives.

"I spent today at the school interviewing all the teachers who stayed late and helped with the cleanup. To be honest, it was difficult for some of them to have confirmed alibis concerning the time of night."

"What do you mean, confirmed alibis?" Lily asked.

"For instance if the person is married, then they have an alibi witness who can attest to the fact that they came home at a particular time. But for people like Brad and Carol and several others who have no spouses or children, they have no alibi witnesses if they just went to home and to bed alone."

"Did you get any sense of anyone lying about their whereabouts at the time of the attack?" Jerod asked.

"I didn't. And of course there's no guarantee

that the attacker was attending the events at the school last night." He looked from Lily to Jerod. "Are you sure neither one of you can think of anyone who would want to seriously harm Lily for any reason?"

"I swear on my life I don't know anyone," Jerod said fervently, not only trying to convince Dillon, but Lily, as well.

"Dillon, we can't think of anyone," Lily replied. She pulled her hand from Jerod's grip and leaned forward. "Trust me, if I knew who was behind this, I'd make sure you could arrest them."

"Yeah, well, unfortunately right now it looks like no arrest is going to happen any time soon." A flash of anger lit the depths of Dillon's eyes. "I hate it when things like this happen in my town. First that nasty doll and now this, and we have gotten no evidence and currently have no real suspects in this whole mess."

Lily looked at Jerod for a long moment, and he knew instantly what she was about to tell Dillon. "There was one other incident between the bride doll and the attack last night."

Dillon sat up straighter. "What are you talking about? You didn't call me about anything else."

As she explained about the boxers and the note, her cheeks dusted with color, and once again Jerod was struck by how pretty she was. Despite the difficult conversation, in spite of the fact that she was clad in pajamas and was injured, she drew him to her.

"You should have called me when you got them. Do you still have the items?" Dillon asked.

"We threw them away," Jerod replied remorsefully.

Dillon frowned once again. "That's unfortunate."

"We weren't thinking," Lily replied. "But now we think the person who left the boxers is also the same person who attacked me."

"From now on, anything you get, anything that is abnormal or strange that happens, you need to call me right away. And for God's sake, don't throw anything else away." Dillon stood. "I'm sorry I didn't come bringing answers tonight, but we're going to continue to work hard on the investigation."

"Dillon, thank you for coming by," Lily said.

"I wish I could have told you something positive." He moved toward the front door. "Jerod, you want to walk me out?"

"Of course." Jerod got up from the sofa, and the two of them left the house.

"I'll tell you, Jerod, this one has me stumped. Everyone I interviewed spoke highly of Lily. She has a stellar reputation both personally and professionally," Dillon said.

"I agree, and yet there's no question that somebody tried to kill her last night," Jerod replied.

Even in the darkness of the night, Jerod saw Dillion's facial features tighten. "Yeah, and I'll tell you what worries me most—somebody tried to kill her last night, and they didn't succeed. So my biggest fear right now is that another attempt is coming."

Dillon's words twisted Jerod's stomach, because he knew they were true. Somebody was going to try again to kill Lily, and he had no clue from who or from which direction the danger would come.

Chapter 9

It had been three weeks since the attack. Lily's stitches had been removed, and she was healing nicely. She'd returned to work, and now she and Jerod had a new routine—he took her to work each morning and picked her and Caleb up when school was over.

The only result of the attack on her was that she'd suffered several nightmares, something she'd never endured before. And they were always the same—a faceless figure chased her down a dark street wielding a big knife.

She now wandered the house, feeling restless. It was Saturday, and Jerod and Caleb were horseback riding. Jerod had insisted she stay in the house with the doors locked. He didn't want her outside at all. He didn't want her vulnerable in any way.

She went into the kitchen and looked out the window to where the two were visible. Since the attack, they never rode the horses out of sight of the house.

The sight of the two of them together swelled her heart. Jerod was the man she'd always dreamed of Caleb having in his life. The father/son bond she saw building between them every day both touched her and scared her.

There was no question she was falling in love with Jerod, and that really terrified her. When she wasn't with him, she thought about him. When she was with him, there was always a tension inside her. It wasn't a bad tension, rather, it was the anticipation of a smile from him, or a touch, no matter how simple. She had no idea how he felt about her. Certainly he'd been kind and caring to her. But that didn't equate love.

She'd entered into this marriage to save her ranch and to have Jerod's baby. It had been a business deal of sorts. She'd known she would have to have sex with him to fulfill her end of the bargain, but she hadn't expected that she'd like it so much.

They hadn't made love since the attack on her, and for the last couple of nights she'd found herself yearning for his touch on her naked skin and wanting him to kiss her until she was mindless with desire.

She wanted her husband to make love to her again, but he didn't appear to have the same level of desire for her. She was afraid that he looked at making love to her as nothing more than a means to an end. She had the feeling she could be any woman who was open to giving him a child.

And that was depressing. She hadn't told him that she was a few days late for her period. Was she pregnant? She didn't know. There had been occasions in the past that she had been a couple days late, but they had been rare. Even though pregnancy was the goal, she was worried that once the goal was met, he'd be done making love with her.

She moved away from the window and instead went to the oven to check on dinner. One of the things she'd discovered about her husband was that he loved Mexican food, so she'd made an enchilada pie for tonight's supper.

She hadn't expected to find love again after her dismal heartbreak over Cody. She especially hadn't intended to find it with Jerod, but now that she had, instead of filling her with joy, it filled her with a strange kind of anxiety and despair.

What if he never loved her? What if her pregnancy ended any growing relationship they had been building. Would their intimacy that had nothing to do with making love suddenly end? She'd begun to feel like he was her very best friend. Would she lose even that when she got pregnant?

A half an hour later, Caleb and Jerod were back in the house, their energy and good spirits contagious as they all sat to eat. "You should come riding with us, Mom," Caleb said. "I'm getting really good in the saddle, right, Jerod?"

"Right." Jerod grinned at Caleb. "Before long you're going to be riding circles around me."

Lily had come to look forward to their dinners, when they came together and talked about their days. These moments over food truly felt like the family time she had yearned for.

There was always laughter, and seeing the happiness in her son's eyes was worth almost anything, including her being in love with a man she suspected didn't and might never love her back.

After dinner they cleared the dishes and returned to the table. Earlier in the week they had gone shopping and had bought several board games they could all play together. Saturday nights had become official game nights.

She recognized now she should have been doing these kinds of things with Caleb all along. She should have engaged with him far more in the evenings instead of allowing him to play his video games alone in his bedroom.

Caleb hadn't even mentioned playing video games in weeks, preferring to spend his evening time with them even if they were only watching television. This was definitely one of the positive new changes that had come with Jerod.

The other positive thing that had come with Jerod was the ranch had finally stopped bleeding money. He'd sold one of their stud bulls to a neighbor for a premium price and had used the proceeds to get in hay for the winter. He still continued to work on getting the books into the computer whenever he had spare time.

For the first time since Cody had left her so long ago, she felt optimistic about the ranch's future, and it was all because of Jerod. For the first time in years, she didn't feel stressed about the ranching business. She believed in Jerod's capability to turn things around.

They played games until it was Caleb's bedtime, and then once he was tucked in, she and Jerod went into the living room and sat on the sofa together. He turned on the television, but instead of watching anything in particular, he gazed at her.

"How are you feeling this evening?" he asked.

"I'm good. Everything is pretty much healed up," she replied. She fought the impulse to lean into him. His scent—one of fresh air and a hint of his spicy cologne—was now familiar and comforting. She wished she felt comfortable enough with him to snuggle up against him, but she didn't.

"I'm not talking about just your physical condition, how are you doing mentally…emotionally?"

"Okay?" She looked at him curiously. "Why do you ask?"

"I don't know if you remember or not, but last night you had another nightmare."

She looked at him in surprise. "I don't remember it."

"I managed to calm you down and you didn't wake up," he replied.

"Oh, I'm so sorry," she quickly said.

He smiled. "Don't be sorry. I just wish this ordeal hadn't given you bad dreams. Are you not feeling safe?"

She laughed. "Short of wrapping me in bubble wrap, I feel very safe with you." It was true. All her doubts about Jerod being part of a scheme to have her killed had dissipated in the time since her attack.

He reached out and dragged a finger down her cheek, the simple touch instantly flooding her with a welcome warmth. "Trust me, if I could wrap you in bubble wrap to keep you completely safe forever, I would." Instant bereavement swept through her when his arm dropped back down to his side.

She released a deep sigh. "Actually, this afternoon I was feeling a bit restless. Despite going to work every day, I'm feeling a bit cooped up."

"Maybe it's because you haven't been able to get out on horseback or move around freely outside."

"That's part of it," she agreed. "I'm just tired of some unknown person having so much power over me and my life."

Once again he reached out and pushed the errant strand of hair away from the side of her face. This time she leaned into the touch. "I know you're tired of the precautions we've been taking, but I would never be able to forgive myself if anything happened to you. Caleb needs his mother, and I need you."

She savored his words. His gaze was intent, and as she fell into the depths, she knew what she wanted more than anything in this moment was for him to take her into his arms and make sweet love to her.

She captured his hand with hers and brought it to her lips. "I'm ready for bed. What about you?"

"Definitely," he replied, and in his eyes she saw a flame that made her excited for the night to come. The only thing she didn't want to think about was if Jerod wanted to make love to his wife because he desired her, or was he simply making love with her to make a baby?

* * *

"Pull it tighter, Rod," Jerod yelled. He held on to one fence post, and Rod had the other end. The fence had been down that morning, broken through by a couple of rambunctious cows overnight.

As they got the fence taut, Jerod used a sledgehammer to bang down his post and then hurried to Rod and banged down that post. "Whew." Rod grinned at Jerod. "Nothing like a little workout to start the day. You know, I've heard some of the other ranchers talking about coyotes lately. I'm wondering if one of them spooked the cattle last night."

"That makes sense," Jerod agreed. "Thank goodness we don't have any calves to worry about right now. I might want to buy a couple of dogs come spring."

"You know Caleb will want to keep any dogs you buy in the house with him," Rod said.

Jerod laughed. "You've probably got that right."

"He's a good kid," Rod said.

"Yeah, he is," Jerod agreed. "I'm going to head out for lunch. Once you're finished eating, I'd like you to start emptying out the gardening outbuilding. I want to trash anything that isn't good in there."

"Got it," Rod replied.

"We'll go through it all when I get back home.

In fact, I'm going inside now to take a shower and then head out."

"I'll be here when you get back," Rod replied.

Jerod headed to the house, and once inside he jumped into the shower. He had made plans to meet Mac for lunch at the café today, and he was eager to touch base with his friend. They had scarcely had a chance to talk to each other since the wedding. And Jerod was missing a little adult male time with a friend.

Once he had changed into a pair of clean jeans and a black-and-blue-checkered flannel shirt, he headed out the door. As he drove into town, his thoughts couldn't help but go to Lily.

Three nights ago they had made love again, and it had been as wonderful as ever. Afterward she had fallen asleep in his arms, but the next morning he'd sensed a change in her...a withdrawal marked by her unusual quietness.

She didn't appear mad about anything. She was just a bit withdrawn. He thought maybe the whole thing of her being cooped up inside the house was getting to her. In any case, he didn't want to pry, and hopefully she would be ready to share her thoughts and feelings with him once again very soon.

This whole marriage stuff was hard work. After he'd run away from his mother, Jerod had spent most of his life taking care of and thinking only about himself. But since he'd gotten married, his thoughts were only for Lily and Caleb. He wanted to attend to both their physical and emotional needs. He wanted to make sure they were happy and safe. And while he was doing everything he could to keep Lily safe, he was afraid she wasn't happy, and he didn't know how to fix things for her.

He pulled up in front of the café and saw Mac's truck already there. He was definitely looking forward to taking some time to visit with his friend. When he walked into the café, he was greeted by the scents of frying burgers and onions and myriad other things that made his stomach growl with hunger.

Despite the crowd inside, he immediately spied Mac in a booth toward the back. "Hey, stranger," Mac greeted him.

"How are you doing, Mac?" Jerod slid into the booth facing his friend.

"The real question is, how is married life treating you?" Mac replied.

"It's been good for the most part. You heard about Lily being attacked?"

"Yeah, I think everyone in town knows about it. How is she doing?"

"She's pretty much healed up physically, but the threat of another attack hangs heavy over our heads," Jerod replied.

"Does Dillon have anything to identify who's after her?" Mac asked.

"Not a damned thing."

"Well, that stinks," Mac replied. "And we both know Dillon is damned good at what he does."

"Agreed, It's just that whoever attacked Lily didn't leave any evidence behind."

Both men turned as Carlee, one of the waitresses, appeared at their booth. She greeted them with her bright smile, took their orders and then left.

"So you and Lily don't have any idea who might want to hurt her?" Mac asked.

"None. All I'm doing right now is basically acting like her bodyguard and keeping everyone I can away from her."

"Is she working?" Mac asked.

Jerod nodded. "I'm taking her to work and picking her up every afternoon. I think she's safe in public places, but I don't want her to be out alone anywhere."

"That's a crappy way to live," Mac said.

"Tell me about it," Jerod replied drily. "So, tell me what's happening at the ranch," Jerod said, wanting to change the topic.

For the next fifteen minutes, he and Mac talked about the Holiday Ranch, and by that time their lunch orders arrived. "Are you seeing anyone?" Jerod asked between bites of his cheeseburger.

"No, I've pretty much given up on dating," Mac replied.

"I just realized out of all the twelve of us guys who came to the Holiday Ranch around the same time, you're the last bachelor standing."

Mac laughed. "I guess you're right. I think maybe I'll always be a bachelor."

Jerod frowned. "Why would you say that?"

Mac shrugged. "I don't know, I'm just not sure love is in the cards for me." He grinned. "I've got my guitar and the horses and the other ranch hands, and if that's it, then I'll be okay. I know why you married Lily. Is there any magic happening between the two of you? Are you falling in love with her?"

Jerod frowned and took a moment to eat one of his French fries. Was he falling in love with Lily? He wasn't sure he knew what love was. Certainly it wasn't anything he'd ever felt in his mother's care. He'd never been in love before, so he had nothing to compare his feelings for Lily with.

"I definitely care deeply about her and Caleb. But to be honest, that's a question I haven't really asked myself. I do know I'm happy where I'm at," he replied. "And I can't think of anyplace else I'd rather be."

"At the end of the day, I guess that's all that's important," Mac replied.

"So, tell me what's going on at the ranch. The new hires still working out okay?" Jerod asked.

"For the most part. Cassie hired on another guy two weeks ago. His name is Brett Davis, but I don't think he's going to be around for long."

"Why not?"

"I think the man has a bit of a drinking problem. Several of us have noticed he smells like booze first thing in the morning."

"Cassie won't stand for that. She and Sawyer have a strict no-drinking-while-working policy," Jerod said. Sawyer Quincy had been one of the original twelve cowboys and he now worked as the ranch foreman.

"Exactly. Sawyer has already mentioned it to Cassie, so I have a feeling Brett's days at the ranch are numbered."

The two visited for a while longer, and then it was time for Mac to get back to the Holiday Ranch and the rest of his workday. The two stepped out of the café, and Mac headed in one direction and Jerod turned in the opposite direction. He nearly bowled over Donna Maddox, the woman he'd dated several months before he'd married Lily.

"Whoa," he said and grabbed her by the shoulders to steady her. "Hi, Donna."

"Jerod," she greeted him with a warm smile. "You're looking well. Married life must be agreeing with you."

"It is. How are things with you?"

"Going well, thank you. I'm definitely keeping busy at the dress shop. I've started seeing a new man from Oklahoma City, and it's going very well."

"Good, I'm glad for you, Donna," he replied. She was a nice woman, and he hoped she found the love she'd been looking for. He just couldn't imagine her being a suspect in the crimes against Lily.

They said their goodbyes, and then he headed back to the ranch. As he drove, Mac's unexpected question about him falling in love with Lily played in his mind.

Jerod had been so busy worrying about keeping Lily safe he hadn't had an opportunity to examine the depth of his feelings for her. And he didn't intend to do so now.

Besides, he had no idea what Lily thought of him. He had no idea if her desire was for him or so she could fulfill her end of the bargain by having a baby. Love had never been a requirement of the marriage, and he'd never believed himself lovable material. His own mother hadn't loved him… so why would any other woman?

He wasn't sure he'd know love if it bit him in the butt. Sometimes he found Lily looking at him in a way that made him want to fall into her soft blue eyes. Was that love? And sometimes he gazed at her, wanting to know her thoughts, everything about her past and her hopes and dreams for the future. Was that truly love?

He shoved all these thoughts away, and for the rest of the afternoon he worked with Rod to clean out the old and broken tools from the gardening shed.

Once again that evening over supper Lily was unusually quiet, and he wished he could figure out what was going on in her head. Was she somehow regretting this whole marriage idea? Had she changed her mind about having a baby and was afraid to tell him?

Finally Caleb was in bed, and it was just the two of them sitting in the living room when Jerod finally got up the nerve to ask Lily what might be bothering her.

"What makes you think anything is bothering me?" she asked.

"You've been unusually quiet over the past couple of days. What's going on? Have I done something wrong?"

"No, not at all," she assured him. She then drew in a deep breath. "Some of my teacher friends are going out Friday night to the Watering Hole, and for the first time in a long time, I'd really like to go with them. In fact, I'm seriously considering it."

He stared at her. What on earth was she thinking? "Lily, you know you can't do that."

She raised her chin, and her eyes narrowed slightly. "Jerod, I'm tired of being a shut-in. I need to get out and have a little friend time."

"Have you forgotten that somebody tried to kill you?" he asked her incredulously.

"Of course I haven't forgotten it, but right now I'm feeling like they succeeded. If I can't go outside to spend time with you and Caleb and I can't spend time with my friends, the person who tried to kill me has already stolen my life." Tears filled her eyes. "I'm so tired of it, and I just want to go out Friday night for a little while." Her tears ran down her cheeks.

God, he hated to see her cry. Her obvious unhappiness stabbed him through to his very soul. "Hey...hey," he said softly and gathered her into his arms. "Don't cry," he murmured against her ear.

She wrapped her arms around his neck and cried into the crook of his neck as he rubbed a hand up and down her back in an effort to comfort her. She wept for only a couple of minutes and then backed away from him and swiped the tears from her cheeks.

"I'm sorry," she said.

"Don't be. I know this has been frustrating for you."

"It's gotten to be beyond frustrating," she replied. Once again she raised her chin. "I'm going to go, Jerod."

"Maybe if I drive you and then pick you up, it will be okay," he said, wanting to make her happy despite being afraid for her.

"No." She shook her head. "I can drive myself there and home. My friends will keep me safe, and I'll probably only stay for an hour or two. All I need from you is to be here with Caleb." Despite the tears a moment ago, her chin was raised once again, and she now looked strong and determined.

"You know that's a given." He frowned thoughtfully. "If you insist on driving yourself, then I'd feel better if you drive my truck. That way people would just assume I'm behind the wheel and not you."

"I can do that," she agreed. She then leaned forward and kissed him on the cheek. "Thank you, Jerod, for understanding."

"I'd still feel better if I could get some bubble wrap for you," he replied, grateful when she laughed.

Two hours later he lay in bed next to her and stared up at the darkened ceiling, worry rolling around in the pit of his stomach and making it impossible for him to sleep.

He couldn't even begin to think of all the things that might go wrong with Lily going out on her own. He tried to tell himself she would be fine. She'd be in a public place with friends who supported her and would look after her.

Still, he wouldn't sleep peacefully again until Friday night had come and gone and Lily was back home safe and sound.

Chapter 10

"I can't believe you're coming with us tonight," Carol said Friday morning before school started. "I was starting to feel like Jerod was never going to let you out of his sight again."

"He's just been overly cautious since the attack," Lily replied.

"You know I haven't really asked you much of anything about that because I didn't want to upset you. So, since you're coming out tonight, does that mean Dillon finally made an arrest?"

"I wish, but no. We don't even have a suspect."

"After all this time? That's stinks," Carol replied.

"What stinks?" Krista walked into the classroom.

"That Dillon doesn't have any suspects in Lily's attack," Carol replied.

"That totally stinks," Krista said and then smiled at Lily. "But you know all your best friends will protect you tonight with our lives." Krista fell into a fighting stance with her hands in fists.

Lily laughed. "Don't you know I'm counting on that."

"We're going to just have a little fun and a few laughs tonight. It will be good for all of us to kick back and relax together," Carol said. "It's been a while since we've all been out."

"Is Regina going to make it?" Lily asked. Regina Fairbanks, one of the first-grade teachers, was usually a fourth when they all went out. She was happily married and had a two-year-old son.

"She's definitely in. She told me a little while ago she couldn't wait to have a little time to herself to escape her son's terrible twos," Krista said.

At that moment the school bell rang to start the day, and Krista and Carol scurried out of Lily's classroom to head to their own. Although Lily had put on a brave face in front of her friends about the night to come, she definitely felt a little bit of trepidation.

She probably wouldn't have made plans to go tonight if she hadn't felt the need to get a little distance from Jerod. The last time they'd made love was when she'd realized the complete and utter depth of her love for the man she had married.

Love was never supposed to be part of this bargain…this…this marriage of convenience. She had certainly hoped she could come to care for and respect Jerod, but she hadn't considered that she would fall completely and hopelessly in love with him. She had truly believed that Cody's betrayal so long ago had made her immune to ever loving again.

She wished she could talk to her friends about her confusing feelings, but she and Jerod had started this marriage on a lie. Now it was too late…too embarrassing to go back and tell her friends the truth about everything.

Throughout the day her mind continued to attempt to work through thoughts about her marriage, her feelings for Jerod and wondering about his feelings for her.

It was going to be difficult to love him, to want all of him…his thoughts, his dreams and his touch, and know that he wasn't in love with her. Could she live with that? She honestly didn't know.

And yet there was Caleb, who loved Jerod like a father. Her son had bonded to Jerod in a way she also hadn't expected. And Jerod seemed to love Caleb. The time Jerod spent with Caleb had cleared up the anger issues that had worried her about her son.

Yes, she could live in a loveless marriage for Caleb's sake. It might be painful, it might feel empty, but she would do anything to make her son happy. And having Jerod as his father definitely made Caleb happy.

Maybe getting out of the house tonight to have a drink with her friends would help to clear her mind. She knew she was taking a chance going out, but she would be in public, surrounded by her friends, and she truly believed the risk of anyone coming after her was minimal.

The day passed, and before she knew it, school was over and Jerod was in the parking lot to drive her and Caleb home. "I know you and Krista are going out tonight," Caleb said the minute they were in the truck. "So, can Henry spend the night with me?"

"That's not a question to ask me," Lily replied. "That's up to Jerod. He's the man in charge of things tonight."

"That sounds fine to me," Jerod replied. "While your mother is having a ladies' night out, we can have a boys' night in."

"Cool. Henry already talked to his mom, and she said it was okay," Caleb said.

"I'll call her when we get home and we can figure out the arrangements," Lily said.

At five thirty they all rode together to Krista's place to pick up Henry. On the way back home, the two boys chattered nonstop about their plans for the night.

"Are you sure you're ready for this?" Lily looked at Jerod in amusement.

"I think I can handle it," he replied with a grin. His grin faded. "But you know I won't be happy until you're back home safe and sound tonight."

"I'll be fine," she assured him. "I'll be in public with friends, and I can't imagine anything going wrong." She reached out and put her hand on his strong forearm. "Don't worry, Jerod."

"I'll always worry about you," he replied.

A soft heat swirled in the pit of her stomach at his words. He always knew what to say to make her feel cared for and loved. She pulled her hand back to her lap. For just a few moments, she didn't try to analyze if he meant it or not—she merely basked in the warmth of feeling loved.

By the time they got home and ate dinner, it was time for Lily to start getting ready for her evening out. She pulled on a pair of black slacks and then a bright pink blouse that she saved for more dressy occasions than work. The blouse had a generous scoop neck and fit tight around her body.

Once she was dressed, she went into the bathroom and put on her makeup, adding a bit more eye makeup than usual. Even though she was a married woman, she still wanted to look her best when she was out and about.

Out and about. The more she thought about the evening to come, the more confident she felt about her own safety. The only time she would be vulnerable at all was driving into town and then coming home. But she had agreed to drive Jerod's truck, and she'd have her cell phone with her if she saw any issues.

In fact, she was feeling good about going out. Let whoever tried to kill her in the school parking lot see her out and enjoying time with her friends. She'd show that person she wasn't going to hide away in fear. He or she didn't get to win.

When she was dressed, she walked out into the living room, where Jerod and the boys were playing cards. Jerod immediately stood from the sofa, a soft smile curving his lips.

"Lily, you look really pretty," he said. "I wish I was the one taking you out to the Watering Hole for some dancing."

"Next time," she said, half breathless by the way he was looking at her.

She took a black suede jacket from the closet and then grabbed her purse. He pulled his truck keys from his pocket. "I'll walk you out." He turned to Caleb and Henry. "Don't look at my cards while I'm gone."

Caleb giggled. "We'll try not to. Right, Henry?"

Lily and Jerod walked outside to the boys still giggling. When they reached Jerod's truck, she turned to look at him. "I want you to understand that having drinks with girlfriends is something I don't usually do. But I need this tonight, Jerod. I just feel like I need to take back a piece of myself."

"I know. Just watch your surroundings and be aware of the people around you," he replied. He reached out and pushed her stubborn, errant strand of hair away from the side of her face. "Just come home safe and sound to me."

She smiled. "That's the plan."

"Do you have any idea what time you'll be home?"

"It's almost seven now. I'll probably be home between nine and nine thirty," she replied. "I don't intend to stay too late."

He handed her the truck keys and then leaned forward and kissed her softly on her cheek. "I'll be waiting for you."

She nodded, the lump rising in back of her throat making it impossible for her to speak. She got into his truck, started the engine and then headed down the lane toward the road that would take her into town.

When he kissed her, when he touched her so softly, so sweetly, it sent a soaring yearning sweeping through her. She yearned for his love. She wanted to hear him tell her he loved her madly…passionately. But she feared that she would never be enough for him. He might respect and care for her, but she worried that the kind of love she wanted from him would forever remain elusive.

As she drove toward the Watering Hole, the most popular bar in Bitterroot, she kept an eye on the rearview mirror. Nobody appeared to be following her, and she began to relax.

She didn't want to think about love tonight. She just wanted to have a few laughs with good friends. She had to stop obsessing about Jerod's feelings for her. It didn't matter whether Jerod loved her or not. Cody had made her realize she would never be enough to keep a man happy. She just hoped that she would be enough to keep Jerod in the marriage and he would continue to love her son.

The Watering Hole was a large, flat building with lighted beer signs blinking in the windows and a large neon sign on the roof. Even though it was relatively early in the evening for the true drinkers and dancers to arrive, the parking lot was already half filled with cars and trucks.

She parked as close to the front door as she could, right next to Krista's car. Krista was in the driver's seat and waved to her. Lily got out of the truck, and Krista got out of her car.

"Regina and Carol aren't here yet," she said. "I

was just waiting for somebody to get here before I went inside. Should we go on in and grab a table?"

"Definitely," Lily replied. She certainly didn't want to stand around in a dark parking lot.

The two entered the building, and instantly Lily's nose was assailed by the scents of greasy bar food and beer, of peanuts and dozens of different perfumes and colognes all trying to compete with each other.

Tall tables and booths surrounded a large dance floor, and a live band was setting up on the stage while the jukebox played a rousing country song overhead.

They snagged a booth, and Lily slid in, pleased to feel protected with the high leather at her back and Krista across from her. "How are you doing?" Lily asked her friend. "I don't feel like we've really had a chance to talk for weeks."

"That's because Jerod seems to be keeping a pretty tight leash on you," Krista replied.

"He's just been worried about me since the attack," Lily replied. "So, what's going on with you?"

"Not much… I've got some things on my mind right now, but I'm not quite ready to share."

"Are you seeing somebody?" Lily asked.

"Maybe," Krista replied coyly. "But like I said, I'm not ready to share anything about it right now."

"Okay, but you know you can always talk to me about anything," Lily replied.

"I know." Krista gave her a bright smile.

At that time Carol and Regina arrived, and then waitress Janis Quincy showed up at the table to take drink orders. Lily ordered a diet soda and the other three ordered cocktails and made fun of Lily for being a lightweight.

As they all caught up on each other's lives, Lily began to truly relax for the first time in weeks. There was a lot of laughter among the four. They had all been friends for years, and there was a real comradery between them.

At eight the live band began to play, and one by one the other women got up to dance.

Lily didn't want to join them on the dance floor. The next time she danced, she hoped it would be in her husband's arms. Instead she was just happy to sit and nurse her soda and watch all the people on the floor.

"Hey, Lily." Brad appeared by the side of her booth. "I didn't know you were planning on coming out tonight. Marriage in trouble?"

"Definitely not," Lily replied and slid to the middle of the booth seat so it was impossible for the man to scoot in next to her. "I just decided to have a few drinks with some of the other ladies from school."

"You know if this marriage thing doesn't work

out with Jerod, I'm still around and available." His pale blue eyes lingered on her for several uncomfortable moments.

"Thank you, Brad. But as I've told you before, I'm very happy in my marriage."

She couldn't help but wonder if it had been Brad who had attacked her in the parking lot. Maybe he secretly hated her for the constant rejections she'd given him.

Carol appeared at the booth and scooted in next to Lily. "Hey, Brad," she said. "Are you harassing Lily again?" Her tone was light and teasing, but she looked at Lily as if to assure herself that her friend was okay.

"I'm not harassing her," Brad protested. "I just stopped by to say hello."

"Okay, hello and goodbye," Carol replied flippantly.

"Okay then, I'll see you both Monday morning at school," Brad said and then headed across the room toward the long polished bar on the opposite side of the room.

"I can't decide if he's really creepy or just a pathetic loser," Carol said when he was gone. "But he's definitely obsessed with you."

"I've wondered if he was the one who attacked me that night?"

Carol's eyes widened. "Do you really think it might have been him? I can't imagine him going that far and actually wanting you dead just because you didn't want to be with him."

"I don't know. I've tried to think of anyone who might have a problem with me, and Brad has been the only one I could think of," Lily replied and then smiled as Regina and Krista came back to the booth.

"Whoo, two dances and I'm exhausted," Krista exclaimed. She sank down in the booth and then sucked on the straw in her drink.

Lily laughed. "That's because when you dance, you really dance."

"That's for sure," Regina replied. "She can wiggle her butt faster than anyone in the entire place."

"Yeah, but it still hasn't gotten me a second husband," Krista replied.

"Speaking of husbands, I'm sure my husband is ready for me to get home and rescue him from our little munchkin," Regina said.

Lily looked at her watch. It was a quarter till nine, and she was ready to call it a night. Hanging out at the Watering Hole had never been her thing, and tonight just reminded her of that.

"I think I'm ready to head home," Carol said.

"Me, too," Lily agreed.

"Well, I'm not hanging around here by myself," Krista said. "In another hour or so, all the men here will just be drunk and stupid."

They settled up their tabs and then walked outside together. "We'll see you two Monday morning," Carol said and then she and Regina headed in the opposite direction of where Krista and Lily were parked.

Before Lily could get into Jerod's truck, Krista grabbed hold of her forearm. "Lily, I really need to talk to somebody. Take a quick ride with me." She looked at her pleadingly. "Please, you know I always think better when I'm driving."

Lily looked at her hesitantly. She really just wanted to get home, but she thought about all the times in the past Krista had helped her through a crisis, and she couldn't ignore it if Krista needed her now.

"Please, Lily. Fifteen minutes, that's all I need. I don't have anyone else I can trust."

"Okay, fifteen minutes, but then you need to get me back here so I can get home," Lily replied.

"I promise," Krista replied.

Within minutes Lily was in Krista's passenger seat and they left the Watering Hole parking lot behind. For a couple of minutes Krista drove in silence, but Lily knew her friend was gathering her thoughts. She'd been on these little drives with Krista dozens of times before.

"I've been having an affair with a married man," she finally blurted out. "And I know I need to break it off, but I love him."

Lily stared at her friend in shocked surprise.

Krista's pretty features looked tortured in the dim light coming from the dashboard. "Uh...who? Who is the man?"

"I don't want to say right now. He's told me how much he loves me, how much he wants me, but he hasn't said anything about leaving his wife and family for me."

"Oh, Krista, you deserve so much better than this," Lily said softly.

"I know, but I love him so much, Lily. I... I can't imagine not having him in my life." Tears began to glisten on Krista's cheeks.

"How long have you been seeing him?" Lily asked.

"Four months and two days," Krista replied. "I'm taking you to where we meet."

Lily looked out the car window and realized they had left the town of Bitterroot behind and were now traveling on a country road. "Where? There's nothing out this way."

"There's an old shed," Krista replied.

"A shed? That's where you would meet up with this man? Krista, what's happened to your dignity?" Lily was appalled by what Krista had told her.

"Dignity? I have none with him, and that's why I want you to go to the shed with me. I'm going to destroy everything in there. I've got to stop seeing him." Her voice raised an octave with her emotion. "Please, Lily…this won't take long. I just need you to help me."

"I'm here and of course I'll help you," Lily replied. She was definitely curious about who the married man might be, but apparently Krista still wasn't ready to share that particular information.

Krista turned once again on a narrow lane that led through a treed area. The old shed was nestled among the trees. The wood was weatherworn, and the entire structure leaned slightly to the left. From the outside it definitely looked like one of the many abandoned outbuildings that dotted the landscape of farming communities everywhere.

"This won't take long," Krista said. "I promise I'll have you back to your truck in fifteen minutes or so." She left the car running, the headlights bright on the shed as she and Lily got out.

The weeds were tall, and Lily couldn't believe this was where Krista met her mystery married man. They certainly didn't have to worry about anyone finding them together here.

Krista picked up a lantern that was hidden in the tall grass at the side of the shed. She turned it on. "Can you hold this for me?"

"Sure." Lily took the lantern.

Krista produced a key to unlock the padlock that held the door. She unlocked it and pulled the door open. "You can go first with the light."

Lily stepped into the shed. The first thing she

saw was the twin bed that took up half the space. The single sheet was twisted and an old blanket made the rest of the bedding. It made her positively sick to think of Krista coming here to meet a married man who probably only saw her as a booty call.

She raised the lantern higher and froze. Pictures of Jerod were nailed to the wall. What in the heck…? She whirled around to look at Krista, who immediately came at her with a knife.

For a moment Lily didn't react. She couldn't. She was frozen in utter disbelief. This was her very best friend. What was happening right now? And then the knife plunged into her shoulder. She dropped the lantern to the floor, where it continued to shine of the walls.

"Krista," she managed to gasp. "Wh-what are you doing?" The woman stood in front of the door so Lily couldn't get out of the shed. She looked almost demonic with resentment shining from her eyes and her mouth twisted in grim determination.

"You're in my way, Lily. I want Jerod, and I'll get him once you're gone." She raised the knife again, and Lily half turned in an effort to protect herself. The knife stabbed into her back and almost immediately stabbed her again.

She screamed and turned back to Krista. She swung a fist and connected with Krista's chin. She tried to hit her again, but Krista flew into a frenzied rage, slashing and stabbing Lily in the arms, in the thigh and God knew where else.

Lily backed up, her heart banging hard and her breaths coming out in painful gasps. "Krista, please stop this now." It was death by a thousand cuts, and Lily could scarcely think with all the pain that sizzled and screamed through her.

Krista backed up a step. "It's done, Lily. And it won't be long before Jerod is all mine." She stepped out of the shed and slammed the door shut.

Lily immediately ran to the door and pushed hard against it. Locked. She banged on it. "Krista, please let me out. Let's talk, I know we can work this out."

"I've already worked it out," Krista replied, her voice barely audible through the shed's wood. "You've told me what a wonderful husband Jerod is to you and what an awesome father he is to Caleb. Henry needs an awesome father, and I deserve a wonderful husband."

"Krista, this will never work," Lily replied.

"Yes, it will. Jerod will mourn you, and I intend to be right by his side, helping him to get over you, and in that process he's going to fall madly in love with me. Lily, you're plain and boring. Jerod deserves much better than you."

Lily couldn't believe this was happening. Of all the people in her life, the last person she would have suspected was Krista. "Did you hang the bride doll off my porch and leave those boxers in the mailbox?"

"Yeah, and you probably know I tried to kill you the night of the science fair. Lily, I've stabbed you enough times tonight that you'll probably die from blood loss. And if that doesn't happen you're going to starve to death, because nobody will ever find you out here. Goodbye, Lily. It was great having you as a friend, but I really need Jerod in my life more than I need you."

Lily banged on the door in sheer panic. "Krista, please just let me out. Please, we can talk about all this."

There was no reply. Lily banged on the door as hard as she could. "Krista!" She screamed the woman's name over and over again. She pressed her ear against the door and heard nothing. There was no car engine running, and she knew Krista had left her here to die.

"Ha... I win," Caleb crowed as he won the hand of poker. The boys and Jerod had been playing for the last hour or so. The coffee table was not only littered with matchsticks and cards, but also bowls of tortilla chips and salsa and soft drink cans.

"One more hand and then it's time for you two to head to bed," Jerod said. It was approaching nine o'clock, and he wanted the boys settled in before Lily got home.

Even though he'd tuck both boys into bed, he knew they'd probably stay up whispering to each other for at least another hour or so. Earlier they had pulled out a blow-up mattress for Henry to sleep on next to Caleb's bed.

Jerod won the last hand and then, as the boys changed into their pajamas, he picked up everything off the coffee table and then cleaned it and placed the flower arrangement that belonged there back in place.

He made sure the kitchen was clean and then went into Caleb's room, where both boys were in their beds. He moved to the side of Henry's blow-up bed first. He pulled the sheet up around the boy's neck. "Good night, Henry. I hope you have nice dreams."

"Thank you, Mr. Jerod," Henry replied.

Jerod moved from Henry's side to Caleb's. He pulled the sheet up around Caleb's neck. "Good night, Caleb. Sweet dreams and I'll see you in the morning."

"Good night, Jerod." Caleb rose up and gave Jerod a hug. As always Caleb's show of affection shot straight through to Jerod's heart. He got up, and when he reached the door, he turned back to the boys. "Now don't stay up too late talking and giggling with each other."

The two boys giggled in response. Jerod stepped out of the room and pulled the door closed behind him. Immediately his thoughts turned to Lily. He hoped she'd had a good time this evening with her friends, but he was eager for her to get home.

He returned to the living room and sank down in the chair. He should be able to hear her when the truck pulled up. It was now almost nine thirty. She should be coming home any time now.

By the time another fifteen minutes had passed, his heart began to beat in an uneasy rhythm. She'd told him before she'd left that she would be home between nine and nine thirty. He needed to relax. She was only fifteen minutes later than what she'd told him.

He picked up the remote and turned on the television. He flipped through the channels, looking for something…anything that would take his mind off the tick of time passing.

By ten o'clock his heart was definitely beating a little quicker. He finally grabbed his cell phone and called Lily. It rang a half a dozen times and then went to voice mail.

Maybe she was having such a good time she had lost track of the time. She might be on the dance floor and couldn't hear her phone. He knew how noisy it could be at the Watering Hole. Just because she was late didn't mean anything bad had happened to her, he told himself.

He waited ten more minutes and then tried to call her again. Same result. It rang and rang and then went to voice mail. "Lily, I was just calling to see where you are. It's getting late and I'm starting to get worried about you. Please call me when you get this message."

He got up and went to the window to peer out. He hoped to see that his truck had magically arrived and Lily was getting ready to come into the house, but of course that wasn't the case.

He returned to the chair and called her two more times. When there was still no answer, his heart began to bang hard and fast in his chest as a simmering panic swept through him.

At ten thirty he finally called Krista's phone. She answered on the second ring. "Jerod, is Henry all right?" she asked.

"Yes, he's fine. I was just wondering where Lily is?"

There was a long pause. "Uh…she isn't at home?"

Immediately Jerod's heart felt like it exploded in his chest and every nerve screamed in his body. "Do you know when she left the Watering Hole?"

"All four of us left at the same time…about quarter till nine. I walked out with her, and we were parked side by side in the parking lot. I got into my car and left, and I just assumed she did the same. Oh, Jerod, she should be home by now." Krista's voice held the worry that now filled Jerod. "What are you going to do?"

"I think I'd better call Dillon," Jerod replied. "I'll talk to you later."

His fingers trembled as he dialed the lawman's number. Dillon answered on the second ring. "Jerod, what's happened?"

"Lily went to the Watering Hole with some friends this evening. She told me she'd be home between nine and nine thirty, but she isn't home. I just spoke with Krista, who said they all left the bar around quarter till nine. She should be home, Dillon, but she's not."

"Let me check things out at the Watering Hole and I'll be back in touch," Dillon replied. Dillon immediately disconnected, and Jerod began to pace the floor.

What could have happened to her? Had somebody carjacked her on her way home? Had she even left the bar? How had this happened? She had been with her friends. Where could she possibly be? Or had the person who had attacked her in the school parking lot somehow attacked her once again? His stomach twisted with fear at this thought.

Questions continued to torment him as he waited to hear something...anything from anyone. He needed answers. He desperately needed Lily to be back here safe and sound.

As he waited to hear from Dillon, each tick of the clock was like a savage stab into his heart. He'd never felt so helpless in his entire life. He wanted to drive up and down the streets, rip open the doors of every house in town until he found Lily and could get her safely home.

Still, he knew the best thing he could do right now was let Dillon figure things out while Jerod stayed here with Caleb and Henry. That's what Lily would want.

Caleb…oh God, he didn't want to have to tell Caleb that his mother hadn't made it home. He didn't want to have to see Caleb's innocent eyes fill with fear. Dillon had to find her…he just had to.

Jerod returned to the window, and as he stared out…waiting…waiting, his eyes misted with tears. He couldn't imagine going to sleep tonight without his body spooned around Lily's. He couldn't imagine waking up tomorrow morning and not being greeted by her sunny smiles.

He rubbed his eyes and straightened his back. No, he couldn't think that way. He was thinking like she was already gone forever, and he refused to believe that.

It was almost midnight when Dillon arrived. A stab of bitter disappointment swept through Jerod when he saw the lawman was alone. Jerod opened the door and stepped outside. "Tell me something, Dillon."

"Jerod, let's go inside," Dillon replied.

"Okay, but I don't want to wake up Caleb and Henry," he replied.

Dillon gave a curt nod, and then the two stepped into the living room. "For God's sake, man. Don't keep me waiting." Jerod stared at Dillon, willing him to have some kind of good news about Lily.

"Your truck is still parked at the Watering Hole, but a couple of my deputies and I went inside and there was no sign of her in the entire building. We began to ask questions, but nobody had seen her leave or knew who she might have left with."

"She wouldn't willingly go with anyone," Jerod replied fervently.

"Did the two of you have a fight before she left here this evening? Is it possible she's at a friend's house and just doesn't want you to know where she is?"

Jerod looked at Dillon in surprise. "Dillon, that's not what's happened here at all. First of all, there was no fight before she left. She just wanted to have a little time out with her friends and then she was coming home. Besides, she would never,

ever leave Caleb here without me knowing where she is."

Dillon frowned. "Okay, what friends was she meeting at the Watering Hole?"

"Krista and Carol Jenkins and Regina somebody. I'm not sure of Regina's last name. I called Krista when Lily wasn't home by ten thirty, and she was shocked Lily wasn't here."

"I'll go catch up with her and the others and see if they can shed any more light on things," Dillon replied.

Jerod stared at him for a long moment. "Dillon, my wife is missing and we know somebody tried to kill her before. We have to find her before…before…" Jerod's voice trailed off as pain shot through to his heart.

Dillon reached out and placed a hand on Jerod's shoulder. "We're going to do everything in our power to find her, Jerod. I've got all my deputies out and searching for her. Right now the best thing you can do is sit tight here and let me know the minute you hear anything from her."

Jerod gave a curt nod of his head. "Stay in touch?"

"Of course," Dillon replied and then he was out the front door once again.

Jerod moved back to the window and watched as Dillon turned around and then headed down the driveway. He watched until Dillon's car lights disappeared into the night.

Disappeared into the night…

Just like Lily.

Chapter 11

When Lily realized Krista had left her in the shed, she crumbled to the bed and began to cry. How had this happened? She hadn't even seen this coming. Had Krista teased her about Jerod being the perfect husband? Absolutely. But so had Carol and Regina, and neither of them had stabbed her and thrown her into a shed to die.

Could she have foreseen that Krista could do... was capable of doing something like this to her? Absolutely not. Krista had never before shown the kind of sheer madness that was obviously hidden away in her mind. Sure, she could say some wicked, mean things at times, but she hadn't ever shown that she could do something like this.

Her purse! Her cell phone was in her purse. She had no idea if she could get a signal out here, but it was worth a try. She looked around the bed and on the shed floor but didn't see her purse. Of course, she had left it in Krista's car. There had been no reason to carry her purse into the shed where she was going to help her friend purge a lover.

As her tears began to subside, her stab wounds began to scream in pain. She struggled to an upright position, set the overturned lamp upright on the small nightstand table next to the bed and started exploring the damage.

She hissed half breathlessly as she shrugged off her suede jacket. "Oh God," she whispered as she realized she was bleeding from all the stab and slash cuts. The pink blouse she had put on to enjoy the night with friends was now splashed with bright red blood.

Warm blood also trickled down the center of her back, but it was impossible for her to see how badly she'd been hurt.

All she knew was that she was in bad shape. Still she pulled herself off the bed. She needed to see if there was some way she could get out of this shed. Krista was right in that nobody would probably ever find her out here. So, she had to find a way out to save herself.

There was nothing inside except the bed and the stand next to it. The rest of the area inside was empty. Despite the worn look of the shed on the outside, there were no holes and no loose boards to exploit as an exit.

In spite of the excruciating pain that ripped through her, she searched inch by inch and finally collapsed back on the bed in failure and exhaustion and horrible pain.

There was a strange fog in her head, and she suspected she was teetering on the edge of shock. Her heart had finally stopped racing and instead beat a rhythm of slow dread.

She looked at the photos tacked on the walls. They were all of Jerod, and it was obvious he hadn't been aware that his picture was being taken. There was one of him on horseback and another stepping out of the community center. Then there were a few more of him walking down the sidewalk in town.

Krista had obviously been stalking him on the weekends when she wasn't at work. Why hadn't Lily seen the depths of her best friend's issues? She'd known Krista was desperate for a husband. She just hadn't known how desperate Krista was to have *her* husband.

As she stared at the photos of Jerod on the wall, she began to weep. He would never know the depths of her love for him. He would never know what a wonderful man and husband he'd been to her.

Her thoughts turned to her son, and her tears raced faster and deep sobs choked through her. If she was never found here, then what would happen to Caleb? Would Jerod continue to raise him on the ranch and be his father? She knew that's what Caleb would want, and she hoped Jerod would want that, too. She desperately hoped that's what would happen.

Still, the thought of never again tucking Caleb into bed, of never seeing his beautiful face or being present in his life as he grew up, nearly broke her. Who would be there on prom night to straighten his tie? Who would be in the car with him when he learned how to drive? Sheer agony at the thought of not being there tortured her.

She felt like she needed to do something to get out, to save herself. With the isolation of the shed, nobody was going to magically come riding to her rescue. If she didn't figure out something, this shed would be her coffin. Years from now maybe somebody would decide to tear down the shed and they would find her bones.

She would scream, but nobody would hear her, and in any case she was too exhausted…too hurt to do anything but lie down on the bed and pray. Maybe if she just rested for a few minutes she could figure out how to survive this nightmare.

* * *

The sun rose in the eastern sky as it always did, but that was the only thing normal about a new day. Lily was still gone, and even though Jerod's eyes felt gritty with a lack of sleep, he didn't intend to rest until he had Lily home.

Dillon had set up his command center in the kitchen, where he'd sat all night long coordinating the efforts of the search and seeing if there would be some kind of a ransom demand. Jerod had spent the night pacing from room to room, his heart racing in anxiety.

He now walked into the kitchen to make a fresh pot of coffee. Dillon looked up as he entered the room. The lawman looked as tired as Jerod felt. "We've checked the entire premises of the Watering Hole. We've interviewed all the women who Lily was meeting, and we've spoken to Brad and several other teachers, as well."

"And nobody knows nothing," Jerod replied flatly. "What was Brad's alibi for around the time Lily left the Watering Hole?"

"He admitted he left soon after he thought she did, but according to him he went straight home and to bed. He didn't see anything happening in the parking lot when he left. But his alibi is weak, so I've got a tail on him. If he goes anywhere today, we'll know where he's at. We're not just going to give up, Jerod," Dillon said softly. "She's out there somewhere, and we won't stop looking until we find her."

"I know." Jerod turned to the counter and quickly prepared the coffee. He then turned back to Dillon. "I want her home unharmed, Dillon. But I keep thinking about the attack on her at the school, and I'm so damned afraid for her."

"I know," Dillon replied with a deep frown. "All I can say is that we're doing everything we can."

Jerod nodded and turned back to the coffee maker. He poured both himself and Dillon a cup and then sank down at the table. "What do I tell Caleb when he wakes up and his mother isn't here?"

"I guess you tell him the truth…that his mother is missing and we're all doing everything we can to find her," Dillon said.

"What a hell of a thing to have to tell a little boy," Jerod said angrily. His stomach muscles tightened. He'd alternated between fear and anger all night long. The problem was he didn't know what to direct his anger at.

He jumped up as a knock sounded on his door. Who in the hell could that be at this time of the morning? Jerod opened the door and was surprised to see Mac.

"Hey, buddy," Mac greeted him. Behind Mac's truck in the drive were several other familiar trucks...the cowboys from Holiday Ranch. "We just wanted to check in. No news?"

Jerod's emotions were suddenly too close to the surface. "No news," he managed to say. "How did you know?"

"Cassie told us. We're all here to join the search, but we need to talk to Dillon so we can be best utilized," Mac said.

Jerod gestured his friend inside and led him to the kitchen, where Mac and Dillon spoke for several minutes. Jerod listened absently. He should have known the Holiday Ranch cowboys would show up to help. They had always rushed to each other's aid. Still, their presence touched Jerod more than he could say.

Within minutes Jerod's ranch brothers were gone, on a quest to find Jerod's missing wife. Jerod returned to the kitchen and drank his coffee, his entire body tied in knots as he thought of Lily.

At nine o'clock the two boys came into the kitchen. Caleb stopped short at the sight of Dillon at the table. Immediately he looked at Jerod. "What's happening?" His blue eyes were wide.

"Your mom got lost last night, and we're trying to find her," Jerod said.

Caleb narrowed his eyes slightly. "What do you mean, she got lost? She's gone out before and she knows the way home." He moved closer to where Jerod sat.

Jerod reached out and pulled the boy into a half embrace. "We don't know what happened to her, Caleb, but she didn't come home last night. Chief Bowie is here to help us find her."

Caleb leaned into him. "What will happen if we don't find her?"

"We're going to find her," Jerod said as confidently as he could. "And no matter what, we're going to be just fine, son. Now, how about I make you and Henry some breakfast and you can take it back into your room?"

He not only wanted to keep things as normal as possible for Caleb, but he was also grateful for something...anything to do. That had been one of the most frustrating parts of the night—his inability to do anything but just wait instead of actively participating in the search.

He decided to make the boys pancakes. When he had a stack ready, he offered some to Dillon, who declined. The boys took their plates and disappeared back into Caleb's bedroom, and Jerod returned to sit at the table and do more waiting.

Lily... Lily, where are you? A vision of her filled his head. He had to believe her heart was still beating with life. To think otherwise was too excruciating to even consider.

Dillon remained on his phone, getting check-ins from his various deputies and marking on a map on his computer where the searchers had been. Jerod sat next to him, trying not to allow his thoughts to go into very dark areas.

At ten o'clock once again a knock fell on the door. It was Carol Jenkins, and she carried in a casserole dish. "Still no word?" she asked worriedly when Jerod let her inside.

"Nothing," Jerod replied. "We've got a lot of people searching, but so far we have no answers. It's like she disappeared into thin air."

"I'm so sorry, Jerod. I can't imagine what happened. I brought over a breakfast casserole. Have you eaten anything?"

He shook his head. "The last thing I feel like doing is eating."

"Let me warm this up and maybe you'll change your mind. You need to eat to keep up your strength until Lily gets home." She carried the dish into the kitchen, greeted Dillon and then set the oven to preheat.

"Now, what can I do to help?" she asked as she turned back to face him and Dillon.

"There's nothing," Jerod replied.

"Why don't you come and sit in the living room with me, Jerod," she suggested.

He could sit in the living room as well as he could sit in the kitchen, and so he followed Carol. She sat on the sofa, and he sank down in the chair. Exhaustion weighed heavy on his shoulders, but he couldn't even think about sleeping without Lily in the bed next to him.

"How's Caleb doing?" she asked.

"He's worried, but thank goodness Henry is here to keep his mind off what's going on."

"Is there anything I can do to help with him? Would you like for me to take him home with me?"

Jerod frowned. "Not right now. I think he needs to be with me. I'd like to keep things as normal as possible."

Another knock sounded at the door. It was Krista. She carried in a dozen doughnuts, and her features held a worried concern. "Still nothing?" she asked Jerod.

He shook his head as once again a wave of despair shot through him.

She greeted Carol and then disappeared into the kitchen. She returned a moment later with a cup of coffee in her hand and a saucer holding two of the doughnuts. "Dillon told me you haven't eaten this morning, and it's already almost noon." She set the coffee cup and saucer on the table next to Jerod. "At least eat these doughnuts and get a little sugar inside you."

"No, thanks," Jerod replied. "I just don't feel like eating anything." Had Lily gotten something to eat? Had she been cold through the night? God, where was she? Why wasn't she here with him?

"You really need to put something in your stomach, Jerod. Lily wouldn't forgive me if I didn't take care of you while she's gone," Krista said.

"Speaking of food, I'm going to put that casserole into the oven." Carol left the living room and went into the kitchen.

"She always makes a casserole for every occasion," Krista said when she was gone. "And just between the two of us, her casseroles are never that good. I figured doughnuts would be the perfect breakfast food for you to just grab and go."

"Thank you, I appreciate your thoughtfulness." What he hoped was that she wasn't going to sit and prattle. He definitely didn't need that. Thankfully Krista got up and went into the kitchen with Carol.

He wanted to keep his thoughts filled with all things Lily. He wanted to think about the sweet lilac scent of her, of the sparkle in her eyes whenever she wanted to share something with him. He wanted to wallow in her laughter and in the quiet conversations they shared in the evenings after Caleb was in bed. He wanted to wrap himself around her each night as they slept.

He'd given Lily more of himself than he'd ever given to anyone. More importantly, he wasn't finished giving pieces of himself to her…and he wanted all the pieces of herself she could give to him. He wanted to know her next thought and share her next burst of laughter. He wanted all her dreams so he could make them come true.

A ruckus suddenly sounded from Caleb's room. It was loud enough that Dillon met Jerod in the hallway and they both hurried down the hall to Caleb's closed bedroom door.

Jerod opened the door and immediately it was apparent the two boys were fighting…and it wasn't a play fight. Henry's nose was bloody, and he had a handful of Caleb's hair and wouldn't let go.

"Take it back," Caleb screamed.

"I won't… I won't. It's the truth," Henry yelled back.

"Hey, hey," Jerod yelled as he grabbed Caleb and Dillon grabbed Henry and they separated the two. Carol and Krista stood at the threshold. "What's going on here?" Jerod asked.

"Henry is saying stupid stuff and I told him to take it back," Caleb yelled as he glared at his friend.

"I'm not taking it back. It's the truth. I know it's the truth because my mom told me and she would never lie to me," Henry yelled back at Caleb. "And then he punched me in my nose."

"That was after you hit me in the stomach," Caleb returned.

"Both of you calm down," Dillon said in his most authoritative voice.

"Now, what did Henry say that got you so upset?" Jerod asked Caleb.

"He told me that you weren't going to be my stepdad anymore, that you were going to be his stepdad. He said that you're going to marry Krista and live with them. I told him that was stupid and a big lie, that it wasn't going to happen."

"But it's not a lie. It's what Mom told me last week. She said Mr. Jerod and her were going to get married and then I'd have a dad and we'd be a happy family."

Jerod turned to look at Krista, his heart suddenly hammering in his chest. "We were just talking… I was just telling Henry that you never knew what might happen in the future." Krista smiled tentatively at him.

"I can tell you for a fact that would never happen," Jerod said flatly. He glanced at Dillon, who was staring at Krista with narrowed eyes.

"Well, you don't have to say it so firmly," Krista replied with a small laugh. "I mean, anything is possible, and I'm not exactly undesirable."

"There's no other way to put it. I would never, ever be interested in you, Krista. You just aren't my type."

Krista's nostrils thinned, as if Jerod's words irritated her. "I'd be a better match for you than boring Lily ever was."

"Krista!" Carol looked at Krista in outrage.

Jerod released his hold on Caleb and instead took a step toward Krista. "What did you do to her?" he asked softly. He clenched and unclenched his fists at his sides.

Krista. Lily would have trusted her best friend. She would have gotten into Krista's car without believing she was vulnerable to any harm. He knew now. He knew now in the depth of his very soul that Krista had done something to Lily.

"My God, Krista...what have you done?" Carol asked, horror evident in her voice.

"You were supposed to be mine," Krista said to Jerod, her voice rising with what sounded like growing hysteria. "I'd already decided that I was going to marry you, that you belonged to me."

"I don't belong to you. I would never belong to you," Jerod replied, his anger barely controlled.

"Why don't you three go into the living room and I'll stay here with the boys," Carol suggested.

Jerod was suddenly aware of Caleb's stricken expression. God, he shouldn't be hearing any of this. As they left the room, Dillon grabbed hold of Krista's arm.

"Now, where is Lily?" Dillon asked Krista once they were in the living room. "Krista, don't play with me, just tell me the truth."

"The truth?" Krista laughed. "The truth is I deserve to have Jerod. Henry deserves to have him as a father." She turned to look at Jerod. "Lily told me what a great man you are and how happy she was having you in her life. We need you way more than she does."

Jerod had never considered hurting a woman in his life, but he wanted to hurt Krista. Still, as he stared at her, he decided to try another avenue to get her to answer the questions he desperately needed answered.

"Krista, I could never consider being with you unless Lily is found," he said, carefully controlling his inner emotions.

"She's probably dead by now," Krista replied. "I stabbed her a bunch of times."

Every muscle in Jerod's body weakened, and he nearly fell to his knees as her words pierced through him with the sharpness of a dagger. He couldn't speak…he felt as if he couldn't breathe.

"Where is she, Krista?" Dillon asked.

Krista looked at Jerod once again. "Once you bury her, do you promise we can be together?"

"I promise," Jerod managed to choke out. It was the first time in his life he had made a promise that he definitely intended to break. "But right now we need to get to Lily and take care of her." An urgency filled him. He needed to get to his wife.

"She's in an old shed about ten miles out of town. I'll have to show you where it's at." Krista's voice held no regret…no remorse whatsoever.

"Then let's go." Dillon grabbed Krista by the arm.

"I'll follow in the truck," Jerod said. There was no way in hell he wanted to sit in a vehicle with Krista. She didn't seem to have any idea how much trouble she was in, but he hoped she spent the rest of her life in prison. If Henry hadn't said anything about his mother's plan for the future, they might have never known what happened to Lily.

As Dillon pulled out of the driveway, Jerod followed close behind in Lily's truck. His was still parked at the Watering Hole. *Lily... Lily...* His heart cried her name.

He was in love with his wife. The realization fluttered in his chest. He hadn't expected it, he hadn't been looking for it, but somehow Lily had worked her way deep into his heart.

Now he was rushing to her, praying that somehow she had survived whatever Krista had done to her, praying that he would get the opportunity to tell her that he was in love with her.

Dillon drove fast, breaking all the speed limits, and Jerod stayed right behind him. His heart beat so frantically he thought it might explode in his chest. The minutes seemed to tick by in agonizing slowness despite the speed of their vehicles. If only Henry had said something last night. So much time had already gone by. Too much time... no, he couldn't think that way.

They turned off on a narrow two-lane road and

traveled on it for a couple of miles and then made another turn onto what was nothing more than a dirt path. They drove through some trees and then he saw it.

The abandoned shed looked like dozens of others in the area. There was no way they would have found it without Krista. He pulled to a halt and was out of the truck door before Dillon parked his car.

The padlock on the shed door kept him from getting inside, but he banged on the wood. "Lily… Lily," he yelled and then waited to listen.

Nothing.

There was no sound from inside the shed. His heart crashed. Were they too late? He turned to Krista, who had just gotten out of the patrol car. "Unlock the door, Krista. For God's sake, hurry up."

"I'm coming… I'm coming," she replied.

When the door opened, what was he going to find? His heart beat so fast he felt nauseous. A combination of fear and dread battled in the pit of his stomach.

Krista unlocked the door. Jerod pushed her aside and instantly saw his wife. She was on a twin bed, surrounded by blood and pale as a ghost. She looked…she looked dead.

Chapter 12

Tears blurred Jerod's eyes as he rushed to her side. "Lily… Lily," he cried.

Her eyelids fluttered and then opened. "Jerod," she murmured.

"Dillon, she's alive," Jerod said with a frantic sob.

"I'll call for an ambulance," Dillon replied.

Jerod looked back at Lily. Her eyes were once again closed. "There's no time for an ambulance. I don't think she can wait," Jerod replied urgently. "She needs to get to the hospital as soon as possible. I'll take her."

Even though he knew it was a risk to move her,

he believed it was a much bigger risk to wait for an ambulance to arrive. "Lily, I don't know if you can hear me or not, but I'm going to pick you up. If I hurt you, then I'm so sorry."

Gingerly he slid his hands under her body and picked her up. Dried blood along with fresh covered her back. She felt cool and clammy to the touch. She was also limp and unresponsive. He turned to leave the shed and was pleased that at some point Dillon had put Krista in handcuffs.

"I'll lead you to the hospital," Dillon said. He grabbed Krista and headed for his car while Jerod carried Lily to the truck. "And I'll call ahead to let them know you're coming."

Jerod placed her in the passenger seat and reclined it as far as possible. He fastened the seat belt around her and then hurried around to the driver side.

Dillon roared ahead, his sirens blaring and his lights flashing. Jerod's attention was divided between the road and his passenger. "Lily, don't you die on me. I'm in love with you and I need you in my life. Caleb needs you. Do you hear me, Lily? I'm in love with you and we need you."

Her eyelids fluttered and she opened them once again. "I'm so confused. Is this a dream? I'm in love with you, too, Jerod, but am I dead?"

"This isn't a dream, honey, and you aren't dead."

She smiled. "That's good." Her eyes drifted

closed again and remained that way for the duration of the ride. Jerod continued to talk to her. He was terrified that she would die before he could get her help.

When he reached the hospital, he pulled up in front of the emergency room, where Dr. Clayton Rivers and two nurses waited with a gurney. They immediately got Lily out of the truck and onto the stretcher, and then they all disappeared into the building in an area where Jerod couldn't follow.

He moved his truck to a regular parking space and cut the engine. He took off his seat belt but didn't get out of the vehicle. Instead a wealth of emotion buried him, and he leaned his forehead onto the steering wheel and began to weep.

Deep sobs racked his entire body. He cried with the relief of finding her and the despair of realizing even though he had gotten her here, she still might not make it.

He cried because she had brought more to his life than he'd ever expected...than he'd ever dreamed possible on the night he'd come to her with his idea of a marriage, and now he was frightened that all of it was going to be stolen away from him.

He finally sat up, scrubbed at his eyes and then left the truck to head to the waiting room. There was nobody else in the room that was lined with plastic chairs and had a vending machine in one corner.

Jerod eased down in one of the chairs, knowing he was probably going to have a long wait. Immediately in alarm he thought of Caleb. Who was taking care of him?

Thank God Lily had texted him the phone numbers of all the women she was going out with the day before. He now checked the text and found Carol's phone number.

He punched it in, and she answered on the first ring. "Jerod, thank God. Please tell me you found Lily and she's okay."

Jerod told her everything and that he was now at the hospital awaiting word on her condition. "Krista's sister came by and picked up Henry, and the last thing I want is for you to worry about Caleb," she told him. "I'll go ahead and take him home with me. I can keep him as long as you need me to. Just promise you'll call me with an update on Lily."

"I promise, and thanks for seeing to Caleb."

"No problem, I'm praying for her, Jerod."

"That makes two of us," he replied fervently.

The two hung up, and Jerod leaned back and prayed that Lily was going to pull through. She had looked so horribly weak, and the idea of the pain she had to have suffered from all the knife wounds nearly broke him.

Minutes ticked by in agonizing slowness. The longer he waited, the more desperate he felt. He had to assume that Krista had been behind everything…the bride doll, the boxers and the attack at the school.

He couldn't understand this kind of madness, although it reminded him of Adam. Adam Benson had been one of the original lost boys who had wound up at the ranch. He'd been one of Jerod's brothers. He'd been smart and funny and had become the ranch foreman. He'd also been a serial killer.

It was only when he'd tried to kill Cassie that Dillon had caught him and Adam's crimes had been exposed. Nobody had seen the madness inside him. It had been a complete shock when it all had been revealed. Just like Krista. It was frightening to realize the evil some people possessed and hid from others so well.

Jerod had no idea how long he'd been sitting when Dillon came through the door.

He sank down next to Jerod. "Any word yet?"

"Nothing," Jerod replied hollowly.

"Krista is now booked into the jail on kidnapping and attempted murder. We'll probably add more charges as the investigation continues. I have a team of men processing the shed as we speak."

"Thanks, Dillon."

"Don't thank me for doing my job. I just can't

believe Krista was behind everything and none of us saw anything the least bit suspicious with her."

"She was the very last person I would have had on a suspect list," Jerod replied. He released a deep sigh. "I still can't believe this happened."

For the next two hours, Jerod waited to hear about Lily. Dillon sat with him for about an hour and then left to continue his investigation. Finally Dr. Rivers came out to speak with him.

Jerod jumped out of his chair, his heart beating furiously. "How is she?"

"She required a transfusion due to her blood loss, but thankfully no organs were damaged. We've cleaned and stitched her up, and right now she's resting comfortably. Thankfully the pregnancy wasn't affected."

The pregnancy wasn't affected? The words thundered in his head.

Lily was pregnant?

Lily opened her eyes and looked around her in confusion. The last thing she remembered was being in the shed and knowing she was going to die. Now she was in a hospital bed with the morning sun just coming up and shining through the window.

She closed her eyes again and thought about Krista. She couldn't believe what the woman had done to her. She'd never seen it coming. She'd believed Krista had killed her...stabbed her to death and she was going to bleed out and die in that shed.

Who had found her? How had they found her? She had no memory of being rescued and brought here. It didn't matter. All that mattered was somebody had found her and gotten her to the hospital.

Emotion rose up in the back of her throat. She wanted to cry with residual fear and with intense relief. But she swallowed hard to keep control.

Pain whispered through her. She opened her eyes once again and saw the stitches down one arm. She knew there were more. She probably now looked like a patchwork doll, held together with stitches and hope.

Her hands went to her stomach. Had she lost the baby? Last week she had finally taken a pregnancy test that confirmed she was, indeed, pregnant. She'd been overjoyed but hadn't shared the news with Jerod yet.

If she was totally honest with herself, she would admit that she'd been reluctant to share the news with Jerod because she feared that once she fulfilled the "contract" terms of their marriage, then their growing relationship would change.

She couldn't think about all that now. She needed to know what Krista had done to her, what kind of wounds she was going to have to deal with. She pressed the button on her remote to summon a nurse.

Within minutes Vanessa Duncan came into the room. She was a young, pretty woman with chestnut hair and blue eyes. She smiled brightly at Lily. "It's so nice to see you awake," she said. "How are you doing?"

"I don't know. Actually I hoped you would tell me how I'm doing," Lily replied.

"Dr. Rivers should be in to see you to explain everything to you. In the meantime, I'll take your vitals." She wrapped a blood pressure cuff around Lily's arm. She got everything done and recorded the results and then looked at Lily sympathetically. "On a scale between one and ten, how would you rate your pain right now?"

Lily frowned. "Maybe around a five."

"I'd say that's pretty good considering what you've been through," Vanessa replied. "Now, how about some breakfast?"

Lily's first response was no thanks, but as she thought about the baby she hopefully still carried, she told Vanessa that she might eat some breakfast.

Vanessa left the room, and immediately Lily's thoughts turned to Jerod and Caleb. She knew Caleb would be fine with Jerod. She also knew Jerod had soothed any fears Caleb might have concerning her well-being. She trusted Jerod with her son's very life, and she knew without a doubt he would be a wonderful father to any other children she might have with him.

Dr. Clayton Rivers arrived to her room before her breakfast tray did. He greeted her warmly. "Lily, how are you feeling this morning?" he asked.

"I hurt in places I didn't know I had, but other than that, I'm feeling okay. I don't remember how I got here or much of anything else."

"You were very weak from blood loss and in shock. Jerod brought you in, and we immediately got to work on you. We had to stitch you up in a number of places, but thankfully none of the wounds hit any vital organs. You also needed a blood transfusion. You're lucky to be alive, Lily."

Her hands moved to her stomach. "Am I...am I still pregnant?"

Clayton smiled. "You are, and the baby is doing just fine."

The relief that rushed through her made tears leap into her eyes. "Thank goodness," she said. The doctor then told her where she was stitched up—her arm, her thigh and across her back.

"You're going to be fine, Lily. If all goes well, I'll probably be able to release you in the next day or two. But it's going to take some time for you to heal. What you need right now is plenty of rest, and I'll keep you comfortable with some pain meds that are safe for you and your baby."

"Thank you, Dr. Rivers," she replied. At that moment Vanessa walked in carrying her breakfast tray.

"I'll just leave you to eat," the doctor said, and then he and Vanessa left the room.

Breakfast consisted of scrambled eggs, toast, a sausage patty and a cup of coffee. The eggs looked brown and overcooked, and the toast was burned around the edges.

She'd just picked up her fork when Caleb came into the room carrying a huge vase of flowers. "Mom, Jerod and I got these for you," he announced.

The sight of her son was welcome, but it was the sight of her husband that suddenly snapped her control and she began to cry. She now remembered staring at his pictures on the shed walls and grieving that she would never see him again.

"Hey, Lily, don't cry," Jerod said. He moved to the side of her hospital bed and pulled her hand into his.

"Yeah, Mom, don't cry. It makes me feel all sad inside," Caleb said. "And I already feel sad inside because of what Krista did to you."

"Don't feel sad," she managed to choke out. "These are happy tears. I'm just so happy to see you both."

"And we're both happy to see you," Jerod replied. There was a tone in his voice, a light in his eyes that felt so much like love it brought tears to her eyes once again. Was she only imagining it because she wanted it so badly?

He pulled a chair up next to her bed and urged her to eat. Caleb stood by her side and eyed her scrambled eggs. "Those look even grosser than Jerod's egg mistakes," he quipped.

Lily's tears turned into laughter. "Yes, but the difference is I'll eat Jerod's egg mistakes, but I don't think I'm going to eat these," she said.

"Do you want me to get you something else?" Jerod asked hurriedly. "I could order something and have it delivered from the café."

"It's okay. I'm really not very hungry right now."

"But you're eating for…uh…to get better," he replied, and his gaze slid away from hers.

He knew.

Dr. Rivers must have mentioned the pregnancy to him, and now it felt like a white elephant in the room. Thankfully Caleb was there to keep the conversation light even as she felt an awkwardness growing between her and Jerod.

Vanessa came in to get her breakfast tray. "It looks like you didn't touch anything," she said.

"Maybe I'll be hungrier at lunchtime," Lily replied. "Caleb, maybe Vanessa wouldn't mind showing you the vending machine next to the gift shop in the waiting room. And maybe Jerod would give you a couple of dollars to get a little snack and a drink."

"I can do that," Jerod said and got out his wallet.

"And I'd be happy to take this handsome young man to the vending machine," Vanessa replied, making Caleb duck his head and smile shyly at her. Jerod handed Caleb some money, and then he and Vanessa left the room.

Lily gazed at the man she had wed in a marriage of convenience. He had saved her ranch, but more importantly, he was the man who had unexpectedly and completely stolen her heart away. "Dr. Rivers told you?"

"He did. What I'm wondering is why you didn't tell me?" There was no censure in his voice, only a soft question.

She stared at him, and all the love she held for him in her heart rose to the surface. "I was going to tell you, but I was afraid that once I was pregnant you wouldn't want me anymore." Tears blurred her vision as she gazed at him. "I… I… This was supposed to be a marriage without love…but…but I've fallen in love with you, Jerod." Her tears came faster. "I'm so sorry, I shouldn't have told you that. I shouldn't burden you with my feelings."

"Lily." He grabbed her hand once again and stood. His eyes were lit with a shine that half stole her breath away. "Lily, don't apologize. I am so happy that you told me that you've fallen in love with me. I've been looking for the right time to tell you that I've fallen madly and passionately in love with you."

Lily's heart expanded in her chest. She searched his features. "For real?"

"For very real," he replied. His face reflected a happiness she'd never seen before. "Lily, I wasn't looking for it. I certainly wasn't expecting it, but I love you with every fiber of my being. When I thought I'd lost you…" He choked up and tears misted his eyes. "I couldn't imagine my life without you."

"But I'm here and I have no intentions of going anywhere," she replied, her heart so full she could scarcely speak.

"If I could I'd pull you up in my arms right now, but I don't want to hurt you," he said, with the threat of his tears gone and happiness once again shining from his eyes.

"Jerod, we're going to have a baby," she said tremulously.

"As important and as loved as that baby is, I need and want you in my life, Lily. You are a beautiful woman, Lily. You are my beautiful, caring, giving wife."

For so long her internal dialogue had told her she was plain and boring and not worthy of love. His words made not only her physical pain, but also the pain of her parents' and Cody's mental abuse disappear as she fell into the sweet softness of his gaze.

"I conceived this baby with love, Jerod. Not because of a contract that we made with each other. I want this baby and I want you, because I love you madly and passionately," she replied.

"I will love you until the day I die and beyond, Lily Steen." He bent down and kissed her. It was a sweet, tender kiss that tasted of his love and his promise of the future of forever love.

Epilogue

Jerod and Lily sat side by side on the porch swing and watched as Caleb rode his horse in the corral. Jerod pulled Lily closer to his side and kissed her forehead and she snuggled closer to his side.

Although the March air was a bit nippy, the sun was bright overhead. Lily was clad in a pale blue sweater that stretched taut around her growing pregnant belly.

It had been almost six months since he'd pulled her out of that shed and they had proclaimed their love for each other. It had been the very best six months of Jerod's life.

When he'd run away from his mother on that

night so long ago, he'd never dreamed he'd find a love like he had with Lily. He awoke each morning anticipating spending the day with her and went to sleep at night with her in his arms.

She was still teaching, but the plan was for her to stop after she had the baby. The ranch had turned a financial corner, and she wasn't going to need to teach anymore. She wanted to be a full-time mother and rancher, and he was happy to be able to give her that dream.

In the past few months, they had done a lot of talking about the negative internal dialogues they had each suffered due to their pasts, and they worked every day to change the voices in their heads that told them they weren't worthy of love or happiness.

He now reached over and rubbed her tummy. "How's my little one doing?"

"She's doing just fine, but I think she wants some ice cream," Lily replied.

"Oh, she does, does she? And it wouldn't have anything to do with you wanting ice cream?" He looked at her teasingly.

"Of course not, I just want to keep baby girl happy," she replied, her eyes sparkling.

"Hey, Caleb," Jerod yelled. "It's time to get the horse put away. Your baby sister wants ice cream."

"Okay, Dad," Caleb yelled back.

Shortly after Lily had come home from the hospital, Caleb had asked if he could call Jerod Dad. It had been one of the most emotional moments of Jerod's life, knowing that Caleb wanted to honor him in this way.

Caleb had been thrilled to find out he was going to have a baby sister, and he vowed to be the best big brother in the entire world. He was the one who had said that a little sister would be nice and then maybe they could give him a baby brother. Jerod and Lily had agreed with that plan.

As Caleb walked his horse into the barn, Lily turned to Jerod. "Happy?"

"Oh, Lily, how could I not be? I've got my woman, I've got my son and soon we'll have our daughter. We have our ranch and a wonderful future in front of us."

"I never dreamed I could be as happy as I am," she said and then smiled. "A handsome cowboy showed up on my doorstep one night with a crazy idea for a marriage. The best thing I ever did was agree to that crazy scheme."

He returned her smile. "And they lived happily ever after," he whispered. He took her mouth with his, and as always her kiss thrilled him and filled him with a happiness, a contentment and a love that he knew would last a lifetime.

* * * * *

COMING NEXT MONTH FROM

H HARLEQUIN
ROMANTIC SUSPENSE

Available December 1, 2020

#2115 COLTON 911: ULTIMATE SHOWDOWN
Colton 911: Grand Rapids • by Addison Fox
When Grand Rapid's most beloved CSI investigator,
Sadie Colton, is in danger, the only one who can protect her
is Lieutenant Tripp McKellar. She's always had a soft spot for
Tripp but she treads carefully, given his tragic past—and hers.
Can she hide her feelings as the threat against her comes
bearing down on them both?

#2116 COLTON IN THE LINE OF FIRE
The Coltons of Kansas • by Cindy Dees
While investigating a cold case, lab technician Yvette Colton
finally tells overbearing detective Reese Carpenter to back off
her work. But Reese is beginning to realize his frustration may
have been hiding softer feelings toward Yvette. As the cold
case suddenly turns hot, he'll have to help manage an invisible
threat and protect Yvette at all costs...

#2117 OPERATION MOUNTAIN RECOVERY
Cutter's Code • by Justine Davis
A random stop leads Brady Crenshaw, a tough, experienced
deputy, to a shocking accident. As he fights to bring
Ashley Jordan back from the brink of death, he discovers
an even greater danger than an icy cliff. It's unclear whom
exactly she needs protecting from—and how deeply Brady
might be involved.

#2118 ESCAPE WITH THE NAVY SEAL
The Riley Code • by Regan Black
Navy SEAL Mark Riley was almost excited to finally face the
man targeting his father—until an innocent civilian was taken
along with him. He didn't expect to brave close confines with
Charlotte Hanover—or the bond they forged together. Now he
and Charlotte must escape a prison island with only their wits
and his military experience to help them!

**YOU CAN FIND MORE INFORMATION ON UPCOMING HARLEQUIN TITLES,
FREE EXCERPTS AND MORE AT HARLEQUIN.COM.**

SPECIAL EXCERPT FROM

H HARLEQUIN

ROMANTIC SUSPENSE

Navy SEAL Mark Riley was almost excited to finally face the man targeting his father—until an innocent civilian was taken along with him. He didn't expect to brave close confines with Charlotte Hanover—or the bond they forged together. Now he and Charlotte must escape a prison island with only their wits and his military experience to help them!

Read on for a sneak preview of
Escape with the Navy SEAL,
*the next book in the Riley Code miniseries
by* USA TODAY *bestselling author Regan Black.*

"Do you remember that summer we turned my mom's minivan into a fort?" Mark asked.

"We? That was all you and Luke." Charlotte closed her eyes, recalling those sweet days.

"You were there," Mark said. "Guilt by association."

"Maybe so." She opened her eyes. "This place could do with some pilfered couch cushions and a hanging sheet or two."

Mark chuckled. "And gummy bears."

"Yes." She rolled her wrists, trying to get some relief from the handcuffs. "What made you think of Fort Van... whatever it was?"

"Fort Van Dodge," he supplied. "You slept in there. I remember your eyelashes."

She sat up and blinked said lashes, wishing for better light to read his expression. "What are you talking about?"

He rested his head against the panel. "Your eyelashes turned into little gold fans on your cheeks when you slept. Still happens, I bet."

Weary and uncertain, she drew his words straight into her heart. She should probably find something witty to say or a memory to share, but her adrenaline spikes were giving way to pure exhaustion. Better to stay quiet than say something that made him feel obligated to take on more of her stress.

"Sleep if you can," Mark said, as if he'd read her mind. "I won't let anything happen."

He clearly wanted to spare her, and she appreciated his efforts, but she had a feeling it would take both of them working together to escape this mess.

Don't miss
Escape with the Navy SEAL *by Regan Black,*
available December 2020 wherever
Harlequin Romantic Suspense
books and ebooks are sold.

Harlequin.com

Love Harlequin romance?

DISCOVER.

Be the first to find out about promotions,
news and exclusive content!

f Facebook.com/HarlequinBooks

🐦 Twitter.com/HarlequinBooks

📷 Instagram.com/HarlequinBooks

📌 Pinterest.com/HarlequinBooks

ReaderService.com

EXPLORE.

Sign up for the Harlequin e-newsletter and
download a free book from any series at
TryHarlequin.com

CONNECT.

Join our Harlequin community to
share your thoughts and connect
with other romance readers!
Facebook.com/groups/HarlequinConnection

HARLEQUIN

HSOCIAL2020